Sir Arthur Conan Doyle

Uncle Bernac

A Memory of the Empire

Sir Arthur Conan Doyle

Uncle Bernac
A Memory of the Empire

ISBN/EAN: 9783337165147

Printed in Europe, USA, Canada, Australia, Japan

Cover: Foto ©Andreas Hilbeck / pixelio.de

More available books at **www.hansebooks.com**

UNCLE BERNAC

A MEMORY OF THE EMPIRE

BY

A. CONAN DOYLE

AUTHOR OF 'MICAH CLARKE' 'THE WHITE COMPANY'
'RODNEY STONE' ETC.

LONDON
SMITH, ELDER, & CO., 15 WATERLOO PLACE
1897

NOTE.

THIS Novel has been re-written and length-
ened by one third since its appearance in serial
form.

A. CONAN DOYLE.

HINDHEAD : *April* 23, 1897.

182

CONTENTS

CHAPTER   PAGE

I. THE COAST OF FRANCE 1

II. THE SALT-MARSH. 21

III. THE RUINED COTTAGE 36

IV. MEN OF THE NIGHT 45

V. THE LAW 62

VI. THE SECRET PASSAGE 77

VII. THE OWNER OF GROSBOIS 92

VIII. COUSIN SIBYLLE 105

IX. THE CAMP OF BOULOGNE 122

X. THE ANTE-ROOM 138

XI. THE SECRETARY 157

XII. THE MAN OF ACTION 170

XIII. THE MAN OF DREAMS 201

XIV. JOSEPHINE 220

XV. THE RECEPTION OF THE EMPRESS . . . 237

XVI. THE LIBRARY OF GROSBOIS 265

XVII. THE END 288

a

ILLUSTRATIONS

HE WALKED ACROSS TO THE WINDOW, AND
LOOKED VERY EARNESTLY OUT OF IT . . . *Frontispiece*

I TURNED TO WATCH THE VANISHING BOAT   *To face p.* 20

IF THEY WERE THE JUDGE AND JURY, IT
WAS CLEAR WHO WAS TO BE EXECUTIONER   „   48

'BUT WHO IS THIS?' ASKED GENERAL
SAVARY, POINTING AT ME. . . .   „   73

SHE ROSE AS WE ENTERED, AND I SAW
THAT SHE WAS TALL AND SLENDER. .   „   94

SHE GRIPPED ME BY THE WRIST IN HER
ANXIETY . . . .   „   118

FOR MY OWN PART I SPRANG READILY
ENOUGH INTO THE SADDLE . . .   „   122

'THOSE FELLOWS ON THE BLACK HORSES
WITH THE GREAT BLUE RUGS UPON
THEIR CROUPS ARE THE CUIRASSIERS' .   „   135

THEN HE PUT OUT HIS HAND AND PINCHED

ONE OF MY EARS . . . . . . *To face p.* 156

'SIRE!' SHE CRIED, 'YOU SAY THAT AN

EXAMPLE MUST BE MADE. THERE IS

TOUSSAC' . . . . . . ,, 200

WE RUSHED IN, WEAPONS IN HAND, TO

FIND OURSELVES IN AN EMPTY ROOM . ,, 276

HE SWUNG A HEAVY CHAIR OVER HIS

HEAD . . . . ,, 284

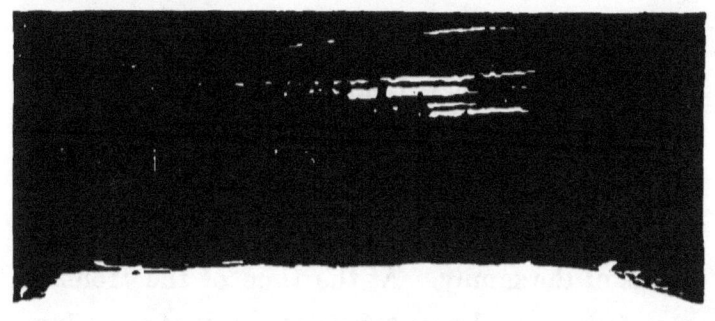

CHAPTER I

THE COAST OF FRANCE

I DARE say that I had already read my uncle's letter a hundred times, and I am sure that I knew it by heart. None the less I took it out of my pocket, and, sitting on the side of the lugger, I went over it again with as much attention as if it were for the first time. It was written in a prim, angular hand, such as one might expect from a man who had begun life as a village attorney, and it was addressed to Louis de Laval, to the care of William Hargreaves, of the Green Man in Ashford, Kent. The landlord had many a hogshead of untaxed French brandy from the Normandy coast, and the letter had found its way by the same hands.

'My dear nephew Louis,' said the letter, 'now that your father is dead, and that you are alone in the world, I am sure that you will not wish to carry on the feud which has existed between the two halves of the family. At the time of the troubles your father was drawn towards the side of the King, and I towards that of the people, and it ended, as you know, by his having to fly from the country, and by my becoming the possessor of the estates of Grosbois. No doubt it is very hard that you should find yourself in a different position to your ancestors, but I am sure that you would rather that the land should be held by a Bernac than by a stranger. From the brother of your mother you will at least always meet with sympathy and consideration.

'And now I have some advice for you. You know that I have always been a Republican, but it has become evident to me that there is no use in fighting against fate, and that Napoleon's power is far too great to be shaken. This being so, I have tried to serve him, for it is well to howl when you are among wolves. I have been able to do so much for him that he has become my very good friend, so that I may ask him what I like in return. He is now, as you are probably aware, with the army at Boulogne, within a few miles of Grosbois. If you will come over at once he will certainly forget the hostility of your father in consideration of the services of your uncle. It is true that your name is still proscribed, but my influence with the Emperor will set that matter right. Come to me, then, come at once, and come with confidence.

'Your uncle,

'C. BERNAC.'

So much for the letter, but it was the outside which had puzzled me most. A seal of red wax had been affixed at either end, and my uncle had apparently used his thumb as a signet. One could see the little rippling edges of a coarse skin imprinted upon the wax. And then above one of the seals there was written in English the two words, 'Don't come.' It was hastily scrawled, and whether by a man or a woman it was impossible to say; but there it stared me in the face, that sinister addition to an invitation.

'Don't come!' Had it been added by this

unknown uncle of mine on account of some sudden
change in his plans? Surely that was incon-
ceivable, for why in that case should he send the
invitation at all? Or was it placed there by some
one else who wished to warn me from accepting
this offer of hospitality? The letter was in French.
The warning was in English. Could it have been
added in England? But the seals were unbroken,
and how could any one in England know what were
the contents of the letter?

And then, as I sat there with the big sail
humming like a shell above my head and the
green water hissing beside me, I thought over all
that I had heard of this uncle of mine. My
father, the descendant of one of the proudest
and oldest families in France, had chosen beauty
and virtue rather than rank in his wife. Never for
an hour had she given him cause to regret it; but
this lawyer brother of hers had, as I understood,
offended my father by his slavish obsequiousness in
days of prosperity and his venomous enmity in the
days of trouble. He had hounded on the peasants
until my family had been compelled to fly from the
country, and had afterwards aided Robespierre in his

worst excesses, receiving as a reward the castle and
estate of Grosbois, which was our own. At the fall
of Robespierre he had succeeded in conciliating
Barras, and through every successive change he
still managed to gain a fresh tenure of the property.
Now it appeared from his letter that the new
Emperor of France had also taken his part, though
why he should befriend a man with such a history,
and what service my Republican uncle could possibly
render to him, were matters upon which I could
form no opinion.

And now you will ask me, no doubt, why I
should accept the invitation of such a man—a man
whom my father had always stigmatised as a
usurper and a traitor. It is easier to speak of it
now than then, but the fact was that we of the
new generation felt it very irksome and difficult to
carry on the bitter quarrels of the last. To the
older *emigrés* the clock of time seemed to have
stopped in the year 1792, and they remained for
ever with the loves and the hatreds of that era
fixed indelibly upon their souls. They had been
burned into them by the fiery furnace through which
they had passed. But we, who had grown up

upon a strange soil, understood that the world had moved, and that new issues had arisen. We were inclined to forget these feuds of the last generation. France to us was no longer the murderous land of the *sans-culotte* and the guillotine basket; it was rather the glorious queen of war, attacked by all and conquering all, but still so hard pressed that her scattered sons could hear her call to arms for ever sounding in their ears. It was that call more than my uncle's letter which was taking me over the waters of the Channel.

For long my heart had been with my country in her struggle, and yet while my father lived I had never dared to say so; for to him, who had served under Condé and fought at Quiberon, it would have seemed the blackest treason. But after his death there was no reason why I should not return to the land of my birth, and my desire was the stronger because Eugénie—the same Eugénie who has been thirty years my wife—was of the same way of thinking as myself. Her parents were a branch of the de Choiseuls, and their prejudices were even stronger than those of my father. Little did they think what was passing in the minds of their children. Many a time when they were mourning a French victory in the parlour we were both capering with joy in the garden. There was a little window, all choked round with laurel bushes, in the corner of the bare brick house, and there we used to meet at night, the dearer to each other from our difference with all who surrounded us. I would tell her my ambitions; she would strengthen them by her enthusiasm. And so all was ready when the time came.

But there was another reason besides the death of my father and the receipt of this letter from my uncle. Ashford was becoming too hot to hold me. I will say this for the English, that they were very generous hosts to the French emigrants. There was not one of us who did not carry away a kindly remembrance of the land and its people. But in every country there are overbearing, swaggering folk, and even in quiet, sleepy Ashford we were plagued by them. There was one young Kentish squire, Farley was his name, who had earned a reputation in the town as a bully and a roisterer. He could not meet one of us without uttering insults not merely against the present French Government, which might have been excusable in an English patriot, but against France itself and all Frenchmen. Often we were forced to be deaf in his presence, but at last his conduct became so intolerable that I determined to teach him a lesson. There were several of us in the coffee-room at the Green Man one evening, and he, full of wine and malice, was heaping insults upon the French, his eyes creeping round to me every moment to see how I was taking it. 'Now, Monsieur de Laval,' he cried, putting his rude hand upon my shoulder, 'here is a toast for you to drink. This is to the arm of Nelson which strikes down the French.' He stood leering at me to see if I would drink it. 'Well, sir,' said I, 'I will drink your toast if you will drink mine in return.' 'Come on, then!' said he. So we drank. 'Now, monsieur, let us have your toast,' said he. 'Fill your glass, then,' said I. 'It is full now.' 'Well, then, here's to the cannon-ball which carried off that arm!' In an instant I had a glass of port wine running down my face, and within an hour a meeting had been arranged. I shot him through the shoulder, and that night, when I came to the little window, Eugénie plucked off some of the laurel leaves and stuck them in my hair.

There were no legal proceedings about the duel, but it made my position a little difficult in the town, and it will explain, with other things, why I had no hesitation in accepting my unknown uncle's invitation, in spite of the singular addition which I found upon the cover. If he had indeed sufficient influence with the Emperor to remove the proscription which was attached to our name, then the only barrier which shut me off from my country would be demolished.

You must picture me all this time as sitting upon the side of the lugger and turning my prospects and my position over in my head. My reverie was interrupted by the heavy hand of the English skipper dropping abruptly upon my arm.

'Now then, master,' said he, 'it's time you were stepping into the dingey.'

I do not inherit the politics of the aristocrats, but I have never lost their sense of personal dignity. I gently pushed away his polluting hand, and I remarked that we were still a long way from the shore.

'Well, you can do as you please,' said he roughly; 'I'm going no nearer, so you can take your choice of getting into the dingey or of swimming for it.'

It was in vain that I pleaded that he had been paid his price. I did not add that that price meant that the watch which had belonged to three generations of de Lavals was now lying in the shop of a Dover goldsmith.

'Little enough, too !' he cried harshly. 'Down sail, Jim, and bring her to! Now, master, you can step over the side, or you can come back to Dover, but I don't take the Vixen a cable's length nearer to Ambleteuse Reef with this gale coming up from the sou'-west.'

'In that case I shall go,' said I.

'You can lay your life on that !' he answered, and laughed in so irritating a fashion that I half turned upon him with the intention of chastising him. One is very helpless with these fellows, however, for a serious affair is of course out of the question, while if one uses a cane upon them they have a vile habit of striking with their hands, which gives them an advantage. The Marquis de

Chamfort told me that, when he first settled in
Sutton at the time of the emigration, he lost a
tooth when reproving an unruly peasant. I made
the best of a necessity, therefore, and, shrugging
my shoulders, I passed over the side of the lugger
into the little boat. My bundle was dropped in
after me—conceive to yourself the heir of all the
de Lavals travelling with a single bundle for his
baggage !—and two seamen pushed her off, pulling
with long slow strokes towards the low-lying shore.

There was certainly every promise of a wild
night, for the dark cloud which had rolled up over
the setting sun was now frayed and ragged at the
edges, extending a good third of the way across the
heavens. It had split low down near the horizon,
and the crimson glare of the sunset beat through
the gap, so that there was the appearance of fire
with a monstrous reek of smoke. A red dancing
belt of light lay across the broad slate-coloured
ocean, and in the centre of it the little black craft
was wallowing and tumbling. The two seamen
kept looking up at the heavens, and then over their
shoulders at the land, and I feared every moment
that they would put back before the gale burst. I

was filled with apprehension every time when the
end of their pull turned their faces skyward, and it
was to draw their attention away from the storm-
drift that I asked them what the lights were which
had begun to twinkle through the dusk both to the
right and to the left of us.

'That's Boulogne to the north, and Etaples
upon the south,' said one of the seamen civilly.

Boulogne! Etaples! How the words came
back to me! It was to Boulogne that in my boy-
hood we had gone down for the summer bathing.
Could I not remember as a little lad trotting along
by my father's side as he paced the beach, and
wondering why every fisherman's cap flew off at
our approach? And as to Etaples, it was thence
that we had fled for England, when the folks came
raving to the pier-head as we passed, and I joined
my thin voice to my father's as he shrieked back at
them, for a stone had broken my mother's knee,
and we were all frenzied with our fear and our
hatred. And here they were, these places of my
childhood, twinkling to the north and south of me,
while there, in the darkness between them, and
only ten miles off at the furthest, lay my own castle,

my own land of Grosbois, where the men of my
blood had lived and died long before some of us
had gone across with Duke William to conquer the
proud island over the water. How I strained my
eager eyes through the darkness as I thought that
the distant black keep of our fortalice might even
now be visible !

'Yes, sir,' said the seaman, ''tis a fine stretch of
lonesome coast, and many is the cock of your hackle
that I have helped ashore there.'

'What do you take me for, then ? ' I asked.

'Well, 'tis no business of mine, sir,' he
answered. 'There are some trades that had best
not even be spoken about.'

'You think that I am a conspirator ? '

'Well, master, since you have put a name to
it. Lor' love you, sir, we're used to it.'

'I give you my word that I am none.'

'An escaped prisoner, then ? '

'No, nor that either.'

The man leaned upon his oar, and I could see
in the gloom that his face was thrust forward, and
that it was wrinkled with suspicion.

'If you're one of Boney's spies ——' he cried.

'I! A spy!' The tone of my voice was enough to convince him.

'Well,' said he, ' I'm darned if I know what you are. But if you'd been a spy I'd ha' had no hand in landing you, whatever the skipper might say.'

'Mind you, I've no word to say against Boncy,' said the other seaman, speaking in a very thick rumbling voice. 'He's been a rare good friend to the poor mariner.'

It surprised me to hear him speak so, for the virulence of feeling against the new French Emperor in England exceeded all belief, and high and low were united in their hatred of him; but the sailor soon gave me a clue to his politics.

'If the poor mariner can run in his little bit of coffee and sugar, and run out his silk and his brandy, he has Boney to thank for it,' said he. 'The merchants have had their spell, and now it's the turn of the poor mariner.'

I remembered then that Buonaparte was personally very popular amongst the smugglers, as well he might be, seeing that he had made over into their hands all the trade of the Channel. The seaman continued to pull with his left hand, but he pointed with his right over the slate-coloured dancing waters.

'There's Boney himself,' said he.

You who live in a quieter age cannot conceive the thrill which these simple words sent through me. It was but ten years since we had first heard of this man with the curious Italian name—think of it, ten years, the time that it takes for a private to become a non-commissioned officer, or a clerk to win a fifty-pound advance in his salary. He had sprung in an instant out of nothing into everything. One month people were asking who he was, the next he had broken out in the north of Italy like the plague ; Venice and Genoa withered at the touch of this swarthy ill-nourished boy. He cowed the soldiers in the field, and he outwitted the statesmen in the council chamber. With a frenzy of energy he rushed to the east, and then, while men were still marvelling at the way in which he had converted Egypt into a French department, he was back again in Italy and had beaten Austria for the second time to the earth. He travelled as quickly as the rumour of his coming ; and where he came there were new

victories, new combinations, the crackling of old
systems and the blurring of ancient lines of frontier.
Holland, Savoy, Switzerland—they were become
mere names upon the map. France was eating
into Europe in every direction. They had made
him Emperor, this beardless artillery officer, and
without an effort he had crushed down those
Republicans before whom the oldest king and the
proudest nobility of Europe had been helpless. So
it came about that we, who watched him dart from
place to place like the shuttle of destiny, and who
heard his name always in connection with some
new achievement and some new success, had come
at last to look upon him as something more than
human, something monstrous, overshadowing
France and menacing Europe. His giant
presence loomed over the continent, and so deep
was the impression which his fame had made in
my mind that, when the English sailor pointed
confidently over the darkening waters, and cried
'There's Boney!' I looked up for the instant
with a foolish expectation of seeing some gigantic
figure, some elemental creature, dark, inchoate,
and threatening, brooding over the waters of the

Channel. Even now, after the long gap of years and the knowledge of his downfall, that great man casts his spell upon you, but all that you read and all that you hear cannot give you an idea of what his name meant in the days when he was at the summit of his career.

What actually met my eye was very different from this childish expectation of mine. To the north there was a long low cape, the name of which has now escaped me. In the evening light it had been of the same greyish green tint as the other headlands ; but now, as the darkness fell, it gradually broke into a dull glow, like a cooling iron. On that wild night, seen and lost with the heave and sweep of the boat, this lurid streak carried with it a vague but sinister suggestion. The red line splitting the darkness might have been a giant half-forged sword-blade with its point towards England.

'What is it, then ? ' I asked.

'Just what I say, master,' said he. 'It's one of Boney's armies, with Boney himself in the middle of it as like as not. Them is their camp fires, and you'll see a dozen such between this and Ostend. He's audacious enough to come across, is little

c

Boncy, if he could dowse Lord Nelson's other eye; but there's no chance for him until then, and well he knows it.'

'How can Lord Nelson know what he is doing?' I asked.

The man pointed out over my shoulder into the darkness, and far on the horizon I perceived three little twinkling lights.

'Watch dog,' said he, in his husky voice.

'Andromeda. Forty-four,' added his companion.

I have often thought of them since, the long glow upon the land, and the three little lights upon the sea, standing for so much, for the two great rivals face to face, for the power of the land and the power of the water, for the centuries-old battle, which may last for centuries to come. And yet, Frenchman as I am, do I not know that the struggle is already decided?—for it lies between the childless nation and that which has a lusty young brood springing up around her. If France falls she dies, but if England falls how many nations are there who will carry her speech, her traditions and her blood on into the history of the future?

The land had been looming darker, and the thudding of the waves upon the sand sounded louder every instant upon my ears. I could already see the quick dancing gleam of the surf in front of me. Suddenly, as I peered through the deepening shadow, a long dark boat shot out from it, like a trout from under a stone, making straight in our direction.

' A guard boat ! ' cried one of the seamen.

' Bill, boy, we're done ! ' said the other, and began to stuff something into his sea boot.

But the boat swerved at the sight of us, like a shying horse, and was off in another direction as fast as eight frantic oars could drive her. The seamen stared after her and wiped their brows. ' Her conscience don't seem much easier than our own,' said one of them. ' I made sure it was the preventives.'

' Looks to me as if you weren't the only queer cargo on the coast to-night, mister,' remarked his comrade. ' What could she be ? '

' Cursed if I know what she was. I rammed a cake of good Trinidad tobacco into my boot when I saw her. I've seen the inside of a French prison before now. Give way, Bill, and have it over.'

A minute later, with a low grating sound, we ran aground upon a gravelly beach. My bundle was thrown ashore, I stepped after it, and a seaman pushed the prow off again, springing in as his comrade backed her into deep water. Already the glow in the west had vanished, the storm-cloud was half up the heavens, and a thick blackness had gathered over the ocean. As I turned to watch the vanishing boat a keen wet blast flapped in my face, and the air was filled with the high piping of the wind and with the deep thunder of the sea.

And thus it was that, on a wild evening in the early spring of the year 1805, I, Louis de Laval, being in the twenty-first year of my age, returned, after an exile of thirteen years, to the country of which my family had for many centuries been the ornament and support. She had treated us badly, this country; she had repaid our services by insult, exile, and confiscation. But all that was forgotten as I, the only de Laval of the new generation, dropped upon my knees upon her sacred soil, and, with the strong smell of the seaweed in my nostrils, pressed my lips upon the wet and pringling gravel.

I TURNED TO WATCH THE VANISHING BOAT

CHAPTER II

THE SALT-MARSH

WHEN a man has reached his mature age he can rest at that point of vantage, and cast his eyes back at the long road along which he has travelled, lying with its gleams of sunshine and its stretches of shadow in the valley behind him. He knows then its whence and its whither, and the twists and bends which were so full of promise or of menace as he approached them lie exposed and open to his gaze. So plain is it all that he can scarce remember how dark it may have seemed to him, or how long he once hesitated at the cross roads. Thus when he tries to recall each stage of the journey he does so with the knowledge of its end, and can no longer make it clear, even to himself, how it may have seemed to him at the time. And yet, in spite of the strain of years, and the many passages which have befallen me since, there is no time of my life which comes back so very clearly as that gusty evening, and to this day I cannot feel the briny wholesome whiff of the seaweed without being carried back, with that intimate feeling of reality which only the sense of smell can confer, to the wet shingle of the French beach.

When I had risen from my knees, the first thing that I did was to put my purse into the inner pocket of my coat. I had taken it out in order to give a gold piece to the sailor who had handed me ashore, though I have little doubt that the fellow was both wealthier and of more assured prospects than myself. I had actually drawn out a silver half-crown, but I could not bring myself to offer it to him, and so ended by giving a tenth part of my whole fortune to a stranger. The other nine sovereigns I put very carefully away, and then, sitting down upon a flat rock just above high water mark, I turned it all over in my mind and weighed what I should do. Already I was cold and hungry, with the wind lashing my face and the spray smarting in my eyes, but at least I was no longer living upon the charity of the enemies of my country, and the thought set my heart dancing within me. But the castle, as well as I could remember, was a good ten miles off. To go there now was to arrive at an unseemly hour, unkempt and weather-stained, before this uncle whom I had never seen. My sensitive pride conjured up a picture of the scornful faces of his servants as they looked out upon this bedraggled wanderer from England slinking back to the castle which should have been his own. No, I must seek shelter for the night, and then at my leisure, with as fair a show of appearances as possible, I must present myself before my relative. Where then could I find a refuge from the storm?

You will ask me, doubtless, why I did not make for Etaples or Boulogne. I answer that it was for the same reason which forced me to land secretly upon that forbidding coast. The name of de Laval still headed the list of the proscribed, for my father had been a famous and energetic leader of the small but influential body of men who had remained true at all costs to the old order of things. Do not think that, because I was of another way of thinking, I despised those who had given up so much for their principles. There is a curious saintlike trait in our natures which draws us most strongly towards

that which involves the greatest sacrifice, and I
have sometimes thought that if the conditions had
been less onerous the Bourbons might have had
fewer, or at least less noble, followers. The French
nobles had been more faithful to them than the
English to the Stuarts, for Cromwell had no luxurious court or rich appointments which he could hold
out to those who would desert the royal cause.
No words can exaggerate the self-abnegation of
those men. I have seen a supper party under
my father's roof where our guests were two
fencing-masters, three professors of language,
one ornamental gardener, and one translator of
books, who held his hand in the front of his coat
to conceal a rent in the lapel. But these eight men
were of the highest nobility of France, who might
have had what they chose to ask if they would only
consent to forget the past, and to throw themselves
heartily into the new order of things. But the
humble, and what is sadder the incapable, monarch
of Hartwell still held the allegiance of those old
Montmorencies, Rohans, and Choiseuls, who, having
shared the greatness of his family, were determined
also to stand by it in its ruin. The dark chambers

of that exiled monarch were furnished with something better than the tapestry of Gobelins or the china of Sèvres. Across the gulf which separates my old age from theirs I can still see those ill-clad, grave-mannered men, and I raise my hat to the noblest group of nobles that our history can show.

To visit a coast-town, therefore, before I had seen my uncle, or learnt whether my return had been sanctioned, would be simply to deliver myself into the hands of the *gens d'armes*, who were ever on the look-out for strangers from England. To go before the new Emperor was one thing and to be dragged before him another. On the whole, it seemed to me that my best course was to wander inland, in the hope of finding some empty barn or out-house, where I could pass the night unseen and undisturbed. Then in the morning I should consider how it was best for me to approach my uncle Bernac, and through him the new master of France.

The wind had freshened meanwhile into a gale, and it was so dark upon the seaward side that I could only catch the white flash of a leaping wave here and there in the blackness. Of the lugger which had brought me from Dover I could see no sign. On the land side of me there seemed, as far as I could make it out, to be a line of low hills, but when I came to traverse them I found that the dim light had exaggerated their size, and that they were mere scattered sand-dunes, mottled with patches of bramble. Over these I toiled with my bundle slung over my shoulder, plodding heavily through the loose sand, and tripping over the creepers, but forgetting my wet clothes and my numb hands as I recalled the many hardships and adventures which my ancestors had undergone. It amused me to think that the day might come when my own descendants might fortify themselves by the recollection of that which was happening to me, for in a great family like ours the individual is always subordinate to the race.

It seemed to me that I should never get to the end of the sand-dunes, but when at last I did come off them I heartily wished that I was back upon them again; for the sea in that part comes by some creek up the back of the beach, forming at low tide a great desolate salt-marsh, which must be a forlorn place even in the daytime, but upon such a night as that it was a most dreary wilder-

ness. At first it was but a softness of the ground,
causing me to slip as I walked, but soon the mud
was over my ankles and half-way up to my knees,
so that each foot gave a loud flop as I raised it,
and a dull splash as I set it down again. I would
willingly have made my way out, even if I had to
return to the sand-dunes, but in trying to pick my
path I had lost all my bearings, and the air was so
full of the sounds of the storm that the sea seemed
to be on every side of me. I had heard of how one
may steer oneself by observation of the stars, but
my quiet English life had not taught me how such
things were done, and had I known I could scarcely
have profited by it, since the few stars which were
visible peeped out here and there in the rifts of the
flying storm-clouds. I wandered on then, wet and
weary, trusting to fortune, but always blundering
deeper and deeper into this horrible bog, until I
began to think that my first night in France was
destined also to be my last, and that the heir of
the de Lavals was destined to perish of cold and
misery in the depths of this obscene morass.

I must have toiled for many miles· in this
dreary fashion, sometimes coming upon shallower

mud and sometimes upon deeper, but never making my way on to the dry, when I perceived through the gloom something which turned my heart even heavier than it had been before. This was a curious clump of some whitish shrub—cotton-grass of a flowering variety—which glimmered suddenly before me in the darkness. Now, an hour earlier I had passed just such a square-headed, whitish clump; so that I was confirmed in the opinion which I had already begun to form, that I was wandering in a circle. To make it certain I stooped down, striking a momentary flash from my tinder-box, and there sure enough was my own old track very clearly marked in the brown mud in front of me. At this confirmation of my worst fears I threw my eyes up to heaven in my despair, and there I saw something which for the first time gave me a clue in the uncertainty which surrounded me.

It was nothing else than a glimpse of the moon between two flowing clouds. This in itself might have been of small avail to me, but over its white face was marked a long thin V, which shot swiftly across like a shaftless arrow. It was a flock of

wild ducks, and its flight was in the same direction
as that towards which my face was turned. Now,
I had observed in Kent how all these creatures
come further inland when there is rough weather
breaking, so I made no doubt that their course
indicated the path which would lead me away from
the sea. I struggled on, therefore, taking every
precaution to walk in a straight line, above all
being very careful to make a stride of equal length
with either leg, until at last, after half an hour or
so, my perseverance was rewarded by the welcome
sight of a little yellow light, as from a cottage
window, glimmering through the darkness. Ah,
how it shone through my eyes and down into my
heart, glowing and twinkling there, that little
golden speck, which meant food, and rest, and life
itself to the wanderer ! I blundered towards it
through the mud and the slush as fast as my
weary legs would bear me. I was too cold and
miserable to refuse any shelter, and I had no doubt
that for the sake of one of my gold pieces the
fisherman or peasant who lived in this strange
situation would shut his eyes to whatever might be
suspicious in my presence or appearance.

As I approached it became more and more wonderful to me that any one should live there at all, for the bog grew worse rather than better, and in the occasional gleams of moonshine I could make out that the water lay in glimmering pools all round the low dark cottage from which the light was breaking. I could see now that it shone through a small square window. As I approached the gleam was suddenly obscured, and there in a yellow frame appeared the round black outline of a man's head peering out into the darkness. A second time it appeared before I reached the cottage, and there was something in the stealthy manner in which it peeped and whisked away, and peeped once more, which filled me with surprise, and with a certain vague apprehension.

So cautious were the movements of this sentinel, and so singular the position of his watch-house, that I determined, in spite of my misery, to see something more of him before I trusted myself to the shelter of his roof. And, indeed, the amount of shelter which I might hope for was not very great, for as I drew softly nearer I could see that the light from within was beating through at several points, and that the whole cottage was in the most crazy state of disrepair. For a moment I paused, thinking that even the salt-marsh might perhaps be a safer resting-place for the night than the headquarters of some desperate smuggler, for such I conjectured that this lonely dwelling must be. The scud, however, had covered the moon once more, and the darkness was so pitchy black that I felt that I might reconnoitre a little more closely without fear of discovery. Walking on tiptoe I approached the little window and looked in.

What I saw reassured me vastly. A small wood fire was crackling in one of those old-fashioned country grates, and beside it was seated a strikingly handsome young man, who was reading earnestly out of a fat little book. He had an oval, olive-tinted face, with long black hair, ungathered in a queue, and there was something of the poet or of the artist in his whole appearance. The sight of that refined face, and of the warm yellow firelight which beat upon it, was a very cheering one to a cold and famished traveller. I stood for an instant gazing at him, and noticing the way in which his full and somewhat loose-fitting lower lip quivered continually, as if he were repeating to himself that which he was reading. I was still looking at him when he put his book down upon the table and approached the window. Catching a glimpse of my figure in the darkness he called out something which I could not hear, and waved his hand in a gesture of welcome. An instant later the door flew open, and there was his thin tall figure standing upon the threshold, with his skirts flapping in the wind.

'My dear friends,' he cried, peering out into the gloom with his hand over his eyes to screen them from the salt-laden wind and driving sand, 'I had given you up. I thought that you were never coming. I've been waiting for two hours.'

For answer I stepped out in front of him, so that the light fell upon my face.

'I am afraid, sir——' said I.

But I had no time to finish my sentence. He struck at me with both hands like an angry cat, and, springing back into the room, he slammed the door with a crash in my face.

The swiftness of his movements and the malignity of his gesture were in such singular contrast with his appearance that I was struck speechless with surprise. But as I stood there with the door in front of me I was a witness to something which filled me with even greater astonishment.

I have already said that the cottage was in the last stage of disrepair. Amidst the many seams and cracks through which the light was breaking there was one along the whole of the hinge side of the door, which gave me from where I was standing a view of the further end of the room, at which the fire was burning. As I gazed then I saw this man reappear in front of the fire, fumbling furiously with both his hands in his bosom, and then with a spring he disappeared up the chimney, so that I could only see his shoes and half of his black calves as he stood upon the brickwork at the side of the grate. In an instant he was down again and back at the door.

' Who are you ? ' he cried, in a voice which seemed to me to be thrilling with some strong emotion.

' I am a traveller, and have lost my way.'

There was a pause as if he were thinking what course he should pursue.

'You will find little here to tempt you to stay,' said he at last.

'I am weary and spent, sir; and surely you will not refuse me shelter.   I have been wandering for hours in the salt-marsh.'

'Did you meet anyone there ?' he asked eagerly.

'No.'

'Stand back a little from the door.   This is a wild place, and the times are troublous.   A man must take some precautions.'

I took a few steps back, and he then opened the door sufficiently to allow his head to come through. He said nothing, but he looked at me for a long time in a very searching manner.

'What is your name ?'

'Louis Laval,' said I, thinking that it might sound less dangerous in this plebeian form.

'Whither are you going ?'

'I wish to reach some shelter.'

'You are from England ?'

'I am from the coast.'

He shook his head slowly to show me how little my replies had satisfied him.

'You cannot come in here,' said he.

'But surely——'

'No, no, it is impossible.'

'Show me then how to find my way out of the marsh.'

'It is easy enough. If you go a few hundred paces in that direction you will perceive the lights of a village. You are already almost free of the marsh.'

He stepped a pace or two from the door in order to point the way for me, and then turned upon his heel. I had already taken a stride or two away from him and his inhospitable hut, when he suddenly called after me.

'Come, Monsieur Laval,' said he, with quite a different ring in his voice; 'I really cannot permit you to leave me upon so tempestuous a night. A warm by my fire and a glass of brandy will hearten you upon your way.'

You may think that I did not feel disposed to contradict him, though I could make nothing of this sudden and welcome change in his manner.

'I am much obliged to you, sir,' said I.

And I followed him into the hut.

CHAPTER III

THE RUINED COTTAGE

IT was delightful to see the glow and twinkle of the fire and to escape from the wet wind and the numbing cold, but my curiosity had already risen so high about this lonely man and his singular dwelling that my thoughts ran rather upon that than upon my personal comfort. There was his remarkable appearance, the fact that he should be awaiting company within that miserable ruin in the heart of the morass at so sinister an hour, and finally the inexplicable incident of the chimney, all of which excited my imagination. It was beyond my comprehension why he should at one moment charge me sternly to continue my journey, and then, in almost the same breath, invite me most cordially to seek the shelter of his hut. On all these points I was keenly on the alert for an explanation. Yet I endeavoured to conceal my feelings, and to assume the air of a man who finds everything quite natural about him, and who is much too absorbed in his own personal wants to have a thought to spare upon anything outside himself.

A glance at the inside of the cottage, as I entered, confirmed me in the conjecture which the appearance of the outside had already given rise to, that it was not used for human residence, and that this man was only here for a rendezvous. Prolonged moisture had peeled the plaster in flakes from the walls, and had covered the stones with blotches and rosettes of lichen. The whole place was rotten and scaling like a leper. The single large room was unfurnished save for a crazy table, three wooden boxes, which might be used as seats, and a great pile of decayed fishing-net in the corner. The splinters of a fourth box, with a hand-axe, which leaned against the wall, showed how the wood for the fire had been gathered. But it was to the table that my gaze was chiefly drawn, for there, beside the lamp and the book, lay an open basket, from which projected the knuckle-end of a ham, the corner of a loaf of bread, and the black neck of a bottle.

If my host had been suspicious and cold at our first meeting he was now atoning for his inhospitality

by an overdone cordiality even harder for me to
explain. With many lamentations over my mud-
stained and sodden condition, he drew a box close
to the blaze and cut me off a corner of the bread
and ham. I could not help observing, however, that
though his loose under-lipped mouth was wreathed
with smiles, his beautiful dark eyes were continually
running over me and my attire, asking and re-
asking what my business might be.

'As for myself,' said he, with an air of false
candour, 'you will very well understand that in
these days a worthy merchant must do the best he
can to get his wares, and if the Emperor, God save
him, sees fit in his wisdom to put an end to open
trade, one must come to such places as these to get
into touch with those who bring across the coffee
and the tobacco. I promise you that in the
Tuileries itself there is no difficulty about getting
either one or the other, and the Emperor drinks
his ten cups a day of the real Mocha without
asking questions, though he must know that it is
not grown within the confines of France. The
vegetable kingdom still remains one of the few
which Napoleon has not yet conquered, and, if it

were not for traders, who are at some risk and in-
convenience, it is hard to say what we should do for
our supplies. I suppose, sir, that you are not yourself either in the seafaring or in the trading line? '

I contented myself by answering that I was not,
by which reticence I could see that I only excited
his curiosity the more. As to his account of himself,
I read a lie in those tell-tale eyes all the time that he
was talking. As I looked at him now in the full
light of the lamp and the fire, I could see that he was
even more good-looking than I had at first thought,
but with a type of beauty which has never been to
my taste. His features were so refined as to be
almost effeminate, and so regular that they would
have been perfect if it had not been for that ill-
fitting, slabbing mouth. It was a clever, and yet
it was a weak face, full of a sort of fickle enthusiasm
and feeble impulsiveness. I felt that the more I
knew him the less reason I should probably find
either to like him or to fear him, and in my first
conclusion I was right, although I had occasion to
change my views upon the second.

' You will forgive me, Monsieur Laval, if I was
a little cold at first,' said he. ' Since the Emperor

has been upon the coast the place swarms with police agents, so that a trader must look to his own interests. You will allow that my fears of you were not unnatural, since neither your dress nor your appearance were such as one would expect to meet with in such a place and at such a time.'

It was on my lips to return the remark, but I refrained.

'I can assure you,' said I, 'that I am merely a traveller who have lost my way. Now that I am refreshed and rested I will not encroach further upon your hospitality, except to ask you to point out the way to the nearest village.'

'Tut; you had best stay where you are, for the night grows wilder every instant.' As he spoke there came a whoop and scream of wind in the chimney, as if the old place were coming down about our ears. He walked across to the window and looked very earnestly out of it, just as I had seen him do upon my first approach. 'The fact is, Monsieur Laval,' said he, looking round at me with his false air of good fellowship, 'you may be of some good service to me if you will wait here for half an hour or so.'

'How so?' I asked, wavering between my distrust and my curiosity.

'Well, to be frank with you'—and never did a man look less frank as he spoke—'I am waiting here for some of those people with whom I do business; but in some way they have not come yet, and I am inclined to take a walk round the marsh on the chance of finding them, if they have lost their way. On the other hand, it would be exceedingly awkward for me if they were to come here in my absence and imagine that I am gone. I should take it as a favour, then, if you would remain here for half an hour or so, that you may tell them how matters stand if I should chance to miss them.'

The request seemed reasonable enough, and yet there was that same oblique glance which told me that it was false. Still, I could not see what harm could come to me by complying with his request, and certainly I could not have devised any arrangement which would give me such an opportunity of satisfying my curiosity. What was in that wide stone chimney, and why had he clambered up there upon the sight of me? My adventure would be inconclusive indeed if I did not settle that point before I went on with my journey.

'Well,' said he, snatching up his black broad-
brimmed hat and running very briskly to the door,
'I am sure that you will not refuse me my request,
and I must delay no longer or I shall never get my
business finished.' He closed the door hurriedly
behind him, and I heard the splashing of his foot-
steps until they were lost in the howling of the gale.

And so the mysterious cottage was mine to
ransack if I could pluck its secrets from it. I
. lifted the book which had been left upon the table.
It was Rousseau's 'Social Contract'—excellent
literature, but hardly what one would expect a
trader to carry with him whilst awaiting an
appointment with smugglers. On the fly-leaf was
written 'Lucien Lesage,' and beneath it, in a
woman's hand, 'Lucien, from Sibylle.' Lesage,
then, was the name of my good-looking but sinister
acquaintance. It only remained for me now to
discover what it was which he had concealed
up the chimney. I listened intently, and as there
was no sound from without save the cry of the
storm, I stepped on to the edge of the grate as
I had seen him do, and sprang up by the side of
the fire.

It was a very broad, old-fashioned cottage chimney, so that standing on one side I was not inconvenienced either by the heat or by the smoke, and the bright glare from below showed me in an instant that for which I sought. There was a recess at the back, caused by the fall or removal of one of the stones, and in this was lying a small bundle. There could not be the least doubt that it was this which the fellow had striven so frantically to conceal upon the first alarm of the approach of a stranger. I took it down and held it to the light.

It was a small square of yellow glazed cloth tied round with white tape. Upon my opening it a number of letters appeared, and a single large paper folded up. The addresses upon the letters took my breath away. The first that I glanced at was to Citizen Talleyrand. The others were in the Republican style addressed to Citizen Fouché, to Citizen Soult, to Citizen MacDonald, to Citizen Berthier, and so on through the whole list of famous names in war and in diplomacy who were the pillars of the new Empire. What in the world could this pretended merchant of coffee have to write to all these great notables about? The other

paper would explain, no doubt. I laid the letters
upon the shelf and I unfolded the paper which had
been enclosed with them. It did not take more
than the opening sentence to convince me that the
salt-marsh outside might prove to be a very much
safer place than this accursed cottage.

These were the words which met my eyes :—

'Fellow-citizens of France. The deed of to-day
has proved that, even in the midst of his troops, a
tyrant is unable to escape the vengeance of an outraged people. The committee of three, acting
temporarily for the Republic, has awarded to
Buonaparte the same fate which has already befallen Louis Capet. In avenging the outrage of
the 18th Brumaire——'

So far I had got when my heart sprang suddenly
into my mouth and the paper fluttered down from
my fingers. A grip of iron had closed suddenly
round each of my ankles, and there in the light of
the fire I saw two hands which, even in that terri-
fied glance, I perceived to be covered with black
hair and of an enormous size.

'So, my friend,' cried a thundering voice, 'this
time, at least, we have been too many for you.'

CHAPTER IV

I HAD little time given me to realise the extraordinary and humiliating position in which I found
myself, for I was lifted up by my ankles, as if I
were a fowl pulled off a perch, and jerked roughly
down into the room, my back striking upon the
stone floor with a thud which shook the breath
from my body.

'Don't kill him yet, Toussac,' said a soft voice.
'Let us make sure who he is first.'

I felt the pressure of a thumb upon my chin and
of fingers upon my throat, and my head was slowly
forced round until the strain became unbearable.

'Quarter of an inch does it and no mark,' said
the thunderous voice. 'You can trust my old
turn.'

'Don't, Toussac; don't!' said the same gentle
voice which had spoken first. 'I saw you do it once

before, and the horrible snick that it made haunted
me for a long time. To think that the sacred
flame of life can be so readily snuffed out by that
great material finger and thumb! Mind can
indeed conquer matter, but the fighting must not
be at close quarters.'

My neck was so twisted that I could not see any
of these people who were discussing my fate. I
could only lie and listen.

'The fact remains, my dear Charles, that the
fellow has our all-important secret, and that it is
our lives or his.' I recognised in the voice which
was now speaking that of the man of the cottage.
'We owe it to ourselves to put it out of his power
to harm us. Let him sit up, Toussac, for there is
no possibility of his escaping.'

Some irresistible force at the back of my neck
dragged me instantly into a sitting position, and so
for the first time I was able to look round me in a
dazed fashion, and to see these men into whose
hands I had fallen. That they were murderers in
the past and had murderous plans for the future I
already gathered from what I had heard and seen.
I understood also that in the heart of that lonely

marsh I was absolutely in their power. None the
less, I remembered the name that I bore, and I
concealed as far as I could the sickening terror
which lay at my heart.

There were three of them in the room, my
former acquaintance and two new comers. Lesage
stood by the table, with his fat brown book in his
hand, looking at me with a composed face, but
with that humorous questioning twinkle in his eyes
which a master chess-player might assume when
he had left his opponent without a move. On the
top of the box beside him sat a very ascetic-faced,
yellow, hollow-eyed man of fifty, with prim lips and
a shrunken skin, which hung loosely over the long
jerking tendons under his prominent chin. He
was dressed in snuff-coloured clothes, and his legs
under his knee-breeches were of a ludicrous thin-
ness. He shook his head at me with an air of sad
wisdom, and I could read little comfort in his in-
human grey eyes. But it was the man called
Toussac who alarmed me most. He was a colossus;
bulky rather than tall, but misshapen from his
excess of muscle. His huge legs were crooked like
those of a great ape; and, indeed, there was

something animal about his whole appearance, for he was bearded up to his eyes, and it was a paw rather than a hand which still clutched me by the collar. As to his expression, he was too thatched with hair to show one, but his large black eyes looked with a sinister questioning from me to the others. If they were the judge and jury, it was clear who was to be executioner.

'Whence did he come? What is his business? How came he to know the hiding-place?' asked the thin man.

'When he first came I mistook him for you in the darkness,' Lesage answered. 'You will acknowledge that it was not a night on which one would expect to meet many people in the salt-marsh. On discovering my mistake I shut the door and concealed the papers in the chimney. I had forgotten that he might see me do this through that crack by the hinges, but when I went out again, to show him his way and so get rid of him, my eye caught the gap, and I at once realised that he had seen my action, and that it must have aroused his curiosity to such an extent that it would be quite certain that he would think and speak of it. I

called him back into the hut, therefore, in order that I might have time to consider what I had best do with him.'

' Sapristi ! a couple of cuts of that wood-axe, and a bed in the softest corner of the marsh, would have settled the business at once,' said the fellow by my side.

'Quite true, my good Toussac ; but it is not usual to lead off with your ace of trumps. A little delicacy—a little finesse——'

' Let us hear what you did then ? '

' It was my first object to learn whether this man Laval——'

' What did you say his name was ? ' cried the thin man.

' His name, according to his account, is Laval. My first object then was to find out whether he had in truth seen me conceal the papers or not. It was an important question for us, and, as things have turned out, more important still for him. I made my little plan, therefore. I waited until I saw you approach, and I then left him alone in the hut. I watched through the window and saw him fly to the hiding-place. We then entered, and I

E

asked you, Toussac, to be good enough to lift him down—and there he lies.'

The young fellow looked proudly round for the applause of his comrades, and the thin man clapped his hands softly together, looking very hard at me while he did so.

'My dear Lesage,' said he, 'you have certainly excelled yourself. When our new republic looks for its minister of police we shall know where to find him. I confess that when, after guiding Toussac to this shelter, I followed you in and perceived a gentleman's legs projecting from the fireplace, even my wits, which are usually none of the slowest, hardly grasped the situation. Toussac, however, grasped the legs. He is always practical, the good Toussac.'

'Enough words!' growled the hairy creature beside me. 'It is because we have talked instead of acting that this Buonaparte has a crown upon his head or a head upon his shoulders. Let us have done with the fellow and come to business.'

The refined features of Lesage made me look towards him as to a possible protector, but his large dark eyes were as cold and hard as jet as he looked back at me.

'What Toussac says is right,' said he. 'We imperil our own safety if he goes with our secret.'

'The devil take our own safety!' cried Toussac. 'What has that to do with the matter? We imperil the success of our plans—that is of more importance.'

'The two things go together,' replied Lesage. 'There is no doubt that Rule 13 of our confederation defines exactly what should be done in such a case. Any responsibility must rest with the passers of Rule 13.'

My heart had turned cold when this man with his poet's face supported the savage at my side. But my hopes were raised again when the thin man, who had said little hitherto, though he had continued to stare at me very intently, began now to show some signs of alarm at the bloodthirsty proposals of his comrades.

'My dear Lucien,' said he, in a soothing voice, laying his hand upon the young man's arm, 'we philosophers and reasoners must have a respect for human life. The tabernacle is not to be lightly violated. We have frequently agreed that if it were not for the excesses of Marat——'

' I have every respect for your opinion, Charles,' the other interrupted. ' You will allow that I have always been a willing and obedient disciple. But I again say that our personal safety is involved, and that, as far as I see, there is no middle course. No one could be more averse from cruelty than I am, but you were present with me some months ago when Toussac silenced the man from Bow Street, and certainly it was done with such dexterity that the process was probably more painful to the spectators than to the victim. He could not have been aware of the horrible sound which announced his own dissolution. If you and I had constancy enough to endure this—and if I remember right it was chiefly at your instigation that the deed was done —then surely on this more vital occasion——'

' No, no, Toussac, stop!' cried the thin man, his voice rising from its soft tones to a perfect scream as the giant's hairy hand gripped me by the chin once more. 'I appeal to you, Lucien, upon practical as well as upon moral grounds, not to let this deed be done. Consider that if things should go against us this will cut us off from all hopes of mercy. Consider also——'

This argument seemed for a moment to stagger the younger man, whose olive complexion had turned a shade greyer.

'There will be no hope for us in any case, Charles,' said he. 'We have no choice but to obey Rule 13.'

'Some latitude is allowed to us. We are ourselves upon the inner committee.'

'But it takes a quorum to change a rule, and we have no powers to do it.' His pendulous lip was quivering, but there was no softening in his eyes. Slowly under the pressure of those cruel fingers my chin began to sweep round to my shoulder, and I commended my soul to the Virgin and to Saint Ignatius, who has always been the especial patron of my family. But this man Charles, who had already befriended me, darted forwards and began to tear at Toussac's hands with a vehemence which was very different from his former philosophic calm.

'You *shall* not kill him!' he cried angrily.

'Who are you, to set your wills up against mine? Let him go, Toussac! Take your thumb from his chin! I won't have it done, I tell you!' Then, as he saw by the inflexible faces of his companions that blustering would not help him, he turned suddenly to tones of entreaty. 'See, now! I'll make you a promise!' said he. 'Listen to me, Lucien! Let me examine him! If he is a police spy he shall die! You may have him then, Toussac. But if he is only a harmless traveller, who has blundered in here by an evil chance, and who has been led by a foolish curiosity to inquire into our business, then you will leave him to me.'

You will observe that from the beginning of this affair I had never once opened my mouth, nor said a word in my defence, which made me mightily pleased with myself afterwards, though my silence came rather from pride than from courage. To lose life and self-respect together was more than I could face. But now, at this appeal from my advocate, I turned my eyes from the monster who held me to the other who condemned me. The brutality of the one alarmed me less than the self-interested attitude of the other, for a man is never

so dangerous as when he is afraid, and of all judges
the judge who has cause to fear you is the most
inflexible.

My life depended upon the answer which was
to come to the appeal of my champion. Lesage
tapped his fingers upon his teeth, and smiled in-
dulgently at the earnestness of his companion.

'Rule 13! Rule 13!' he kept repeating, in
that exasperating voice of his.

'I will take all responsibility.'

'I'll tell you what, mister,' said Toussac, in his
savage voice. 'There's another rule besides Rule
13, and that's the one that says that if any man
shelters an offender he shall be treated as if he was
himself guilty of the offence.'

This attack did not shake the serenity of my
champion in the least.

'You are an excellent man of action, Toussac,'
said he calmly; 'but when it comes to choosing
the right course, you must leave it to wiser heads
than your own.'

His air of tranquil superiority seemed to daunt
the fierce creature who held me. He shrugged his
huge shoulders in silent dissent.

'As to you, Lucien,' my friend continued, 'I am surprised, considering the position to which you aspire in my family, that you should for an instant stand in the way of any wish which I may express. If you have grasped the true principles of liberty, and if you are privileged to be one of the small band who have never despaired of the republic, to whom is it that you owe it?'

'Yes, yes, Charles; I acknowledge what you say,' the young man answered, with much agitation. 'I am sure that I should be the last to oppose any wish which you might express, but in this case I fear lest your tenderness of heart may be leading you astray. By all means ask him any questions that you like; but it seems to me that there can be only one end to the matter.'

So I thought also; for, with the full secret of these desperate men in my possession, what hope was there that they would ever suffer me to leave the hut alive? And yet, so sweet is human life, and so dear a respite, be it ever so short a one, that when that murderous hand was taken from my chin I heard a sudden chiming of little bells, and the lamp blazed up into a strange fantastic blur.

It was but for a moment, and then my mind was clear again, and I was looking up at the strange gaunt face of my examiner.

'Whence have you come ? ' he asked.

'From England.'

'But you are French ? '

'Yes.'

'When did you arrive ? '

'To-night.'

'How ? '

'In a lugger from Dover.'

'The fellow is speaking the truth,' growled Toussac. 'Yes, I'll say that for him, that he is speaking the truth. We saw the lugger, and some-one was landed from it just after the boat that brought me over pushed off.'

I remembered that boat, which had been the first thing which I had seen upon the coast of France. How little I had thought what it would mean to me !

And now my advocate began asking questions—vague, useless questions—in a slow, hesitating fashion which set Toussac grumbling. This cross-examination appeared to me to be a useless farce ;

and yet there was a certain eagerness and intensity
in my questioner's manner which gave me the
assurance that he had some end in view. Was
it merely that he wished to gain time? Time for
what? And then, suddenly, with that quick per-
ception which comes upon those whose nerves are
strained by an extremity of danger, I became convinced that he really was awaiting something—that
he was tense with expectation. I read it upon his
drawn face, upon his sidelong head with his ear
scooped into his hand, above all in his twitching,
restless eyes. He expected an interruption, and he
was talking, talking, talking, in order to gain time
for it. I was as sure of it as if he had whispered
his secret in my ear, and down in my numb, cold
heart a warm little spring of hope began to bubble
and run.

But Toussac had chafed at all this word-fencing,
and now with an oath he broke in upon our dia-
logue.

'I have had enough of this!' he cried. 'It
is not for child's play of this sort that I risked
my head in coming over here. Have we nothing
better to talk about than this fellow? Do you sup-

pose I came from London to listen to your fine
phrases? Have done with it, I say, and get to
business.'

'Very good,' said my champion. 'There's an
excellent little cupboard here which makes as fine
a prison as one could wish for. Let us put him in
here, and pass on to business. We can deal with
him when we have finished.'

'And have him overhear all that we say,' said
Lesage.

'I don't know what the devil has come over
you,' cried Toussac, turning suspicious eyes upon
my protector. 'I never knew you squeamish
before, and certainly you were not backward in the
affair of the man from Bow Street. This fellow
has our secret, and he must either die, or we shall
see him at our trial. What is the sense of arranging a plot, and then at the last moment turning a
man loose who will ruin us all? Let us snap his
neck and have done with it.'

The great hairy hands were stretched towards
me again, but Lesage had sprung suddenly to his
feet. His face had turned very white, and he
stood listening with his forefinger up and his head

slanted. It was a long, thin, delicate hand, and it was quivering like a leaf in the wind.

'I heard something,' he whispered.

'And I,' said the older man.

'What was it?'

'Silence. Listen!'

For a minute or more we all stayed with straining ears while the wind still whimpered in the chimney or rattled the crazy window.

'It was nothing,' said Lesage at last, with a nervous laugh. 'The storm makes curious sounds sometimes.'

'I heard nothing,' said Toussac.

'Hush!' cried the other. 'There it is again!'

A clear rising cry floated high above the wailing of the storm; a wild, musical cry, beginning on a low note, and thrilling swiftly up to a keen, sharp-edged howl.

'A hound!'

'They are following us!'

Lesage dashed to the fireplace, and I saw him thrust his papers into the blaze and grind them down with his heel.

Toussac seized the wood-axe which leaned

against the wall. The thin man dragged the pile of decayed netting from the corner, and opened a small wooden screen, which shut off a low recess.

'In here,' he whispered, 'quick!'

And then, as I scrambled into my refuge, I heard him say to the others that I would be safe there, and that they could lay their hands upon me when they wished.

CHAPTER V

THE LAW

Thr. cupboard—for it was little more—into which
I had been hurried was low and narrow, and I felt
in the darkness that it was heaped with peculiar
round wickerwork baskets, the nature of which I
could by no means imagine, although I discovered
afterwards that they were lobster traps. The only
light which entered was through the cracks of the
old broken door, but these were so wide and numerous that I could see the whole of the room which
I had just quitted. Sick and faint, with the shadow
of death still clouding my wits, I was none the less
fascinated by the scene which lay before me.

My thin friend, with the same prim composure
upon his emaciated face, had seated himself again
upon the box. With his hands clasped round one
of his knees he was rocking slowly backwards and
forwards; and I noticed, in the lamplight, that his

jaw muscles were contracting rhythmically, like the gills of a fish. Beside him stood Lesage, his white face glistening with moisture and his loose lip quivering with fear. Every now and then he would make a vigorous attempt to compose his features, but after each rally a fresh wave of terror would sweep everything before it, and set him shaking once more. As to Toussac, he stood before the fire, a magnificent figure, with the axe held down by his leg, and his head thrown back in defiance, so that his great black beard bristled straight out in front of him. He said not a word, but every fibre of his body was braced for a struggle. Then, as the howl of the hound rose louder and clearer from the marsh outside, he ran forward and threw open the door.

'No, no, keep the dog out!' cried Lesage in an agony of apprehension.

'You fool, our only chance is to kill it.'

'But it is in leash.'

'If it is in leash nothing can save us. But if, as I think, it is running free, then we may escape yet.'

Lesage cowered up against the table, with his

agonised eyes fixed upon the blue-black square of
the door. The man who had befriended me still
swayed his body about with a singular half-smile
upon his face. His skinny hand was twitching at
the frill of his shirt, and I conjectured that he
held some weapon concealed there. Toussac
stood between them and the open door, and, much
as I feared and loathed him, I could not take my
eyes from his gallant figure. As to myself, I was
so much occupied by the singular drama before
me, and by the impending fate of those three men
of the cottage, that all thought of my own fortunes
had passed completely out of my mind. On this
mean stage a terrible all-absorbing drama was
being played, and I, crouching in a squalid recess,
was to be the sole spectator of it. I could but hold
my breath and wait and watch.

And suddenly I became conscious that they
could all three see something which was invisible
to me. I read it from their tense faces and their
staring eyes. Toussac swung his axe over his
shoulder and poised himself for a blow. Lesage
cowered away and put one hand between his eyes
and the open door. The other ceased swinging

his spindle legs and sat like a little brown image upon the edge of his box. There was a moist pattering of feet, a yellow streak shot through the doorway, and Toussac lashed at it as I have seen an English cricketer strike at a ball. His aim was true, for he buried the head of the hatchet in the creature's throat, but the force of his blow shattered his weapon, and the weight of the hound carried him backwards on to the floor. Over they rolled and over, the hairy man and the hairy dog, growling and worrying in a bestial combat. He was fumbling at the animal's throat, and I could not see what he was doing, until it gave a sudden sharp yelp of pain, and there was a rending sound like the tearing of canvas. The man staggered up with his hands dripping, and the tawny mass with the blotch of crimson lay motionless upon the floor.

'Now!' cried Toussac in a voice of thunder, 'now!' and he rushed from the hut.

Lesage had shrunk away into the corner in a frenzy of fear whilst Toussac had been killing the hound, but now he raised his agonised face, which was as wet as if he had dipped it into a basin.

'Yes, yes,' he cried; 'we must fly, Charles.

F

The hound has left the police behind, and we may still escape.'

But the other, with the same imperturbable face, motionless save for the rhythm of his jaw muscles, walked quietly over and closed the door upon the inside.

'I think, friend Lucien,' said he in his quiet voice, 'that you had best stay where you are.'

Lesage looked at him with amazement gradually replacing terror upon his pallid features.

'But you do not understand, Charles,' he cried.

'Oh, yes, I think I do,' said the other, smiling.

'They may be here in a few minutes. The hound has slipped its leash, you see, and has left them behind in the marsh; but they are sure to come here, for there is no other cottage but this.'

'They are sure to come here.'

'Well, then, let us fly. In the darkness we may yet escape.'

'No; we shall stay where we are.'

'Madman, you may sacrifice your own life, but not mine. Stay if you wish, but for my part I am going.'

He ran towards the door with a foolish, helpless

flapping of his hands, but the other sprang in front of him with so determined a gesture of authority that the younger man staggered back from it as from a blow.

'You fool!' said his companion. 'You poor miserable dupe!'

Lesage's mouth opened, and he stood staring with his knees bent and his spread-fingered hands up, the most hideous picture of fear that I have ever seen.

'You, Charles, you!' he stammered, hawking up each word.

'Yes, me,' said the other, smiling grimly.

'A police agent all the time! You who were the very soul of our society! You who were in our inmost council! You who led us on! Oh, Charles, you have not the heart! I think I hear them coming, Charles. Let me pass; I beg and implore you to let me pass.'

The granite face shook slowly from side to side.

'But why me? Why not Toussac?'

'If the dog had crippled Toussac, why then I might have had you both. But friend Toussac is rather vigorous for a thin little fellow like me.

No, no, my good Lucien, you are destined to be the
trophy of my bow and my spear, and you must
reconcile yourself to the fact.'

Lesage slapped his forehead as if to assure
himself that he was not dreaming.

' A police agent ! ' he repeated, ' Charles a police
agent ! '

' I thought it would surprise you.'

' But you were the most republican of us all.
We were none of us advanced enough for you.
How often have we gathered round you, Charles,
to listen to your philosophy ! And there is Sibylle,
too ! Don't tell me that Sibylle was a police spy
also. But you are joking, Charles. Say that you
are joking ! '

The man relaxed his grim features, and his eyes
puckered with amusement.

' Your astonishment is very flattering,' said he.
' I confess that I thought that I played my part
rather cleverly. It is not my fault that these
bunglers unleashed their hound, but at least I shall
have the credit of having made a single-handed
capture of one very desperate and dangerous
conspirator.' He smiled drily at this description

of his prisoner. 'The Emperor knows how to reward his friends,' he added, 'and also how to punish his enemies.'

All this time he had held his hand in his bosom, and now he drew it out so far as to show the brass gleam of a pistol butt.

'It is no use,' said he, in answer to some look in the other's eye. 'You stay in the hut, alive or dead.'

Lesage put his hands to his face and began to cry with loud, helpless sobbings.

'Why, you have been worse than any of us, Charles,' he moaned. 'It was you who told Toussac to kill the man from Bow Street, and it was you also who set fire to the house in the Rue Basse de la Rampart. And now you turn on us!'

'I did that because I wished to be the one to throw light upon it all—and at the proper moment.'

'That is very fine, Charles, but what will be thought about that when I make it all public in my own defence? How can you explain all that to your Emperor? There is still time to prevent my telling all that I know about you.'

'Well, really, I think that you are right, my friend,' said the other, drawing out his pistol and cocking it. 'Perhaps I *did* go a little beyond my instructions in one or two points, and, as you very properly remark, there is still time to set it right. It is a matter of detail whether I give you up living or give you up dead, and I think that, on the whole, it had better be dead.'

It had been horrible to see Toussac tear the throat out of the hound, but it had not made my flesh creep as it crept now. Pity was mingled with my disgust for this unfortunate young man, who had been fitted by Nature for the life of a retired student or of a dreaming poet, but who had been dragged by stronger wills than his own into a part which no child could be more incapable of playing. I forgave him the trick by which he had caught me and the selfish fears to which he had been willing to sacrifice me. He had flung himself down upon the ground, and floundered about in a convulsion of terror, whilst his terrible little companion, with his cynical smile, stood over him with his pistol in his hand. He played with the helpless panting coward as a cat might with a mouse; but I read in his inexorable eyes that it was no jest, and his finger seemed to be already tightening upon his trigger. Full of horror at so cold-blooded a murder, I pushed open my crazy cupboard, and had rushed out to plead for the victim, when there came a buzz of voices and a clanking of steel from without. With a stentorian shout of 'In the name of the Emperor!' a single violent wrench tore the door of the hut from its hinges.

It was still blowing hard, and through the open doorway I could see a thick cluster of mounted men, with plumes slanted and mantles flapping, the rain shining upon their shoulders. At the side the light from the hut struck upon the heads of two beautiful horses, and upon the heavy red-toupeed busbies of the hussars who stood at their heads. In the doorway stood another hussar—a man of high rank, as could be seen from the richness of his dress and the distinction of his bearing. He was booted to the knees, with a uniform of light blue and silver, which his tall, slim, light-cavalry figure suited to a marvel. I could not but admire the way in which he carried himself, for he never deigned to draw the sword

which shone at his side, but he stood in the doorway glancing round the blood-bespattered hut, and
staring at its occupants with a very cool and alert
expression. He had a handsome face, pale and
clear-cut, with a bristling moustache, which cut
across the brass chin-chain of his busby.

'Well,' said he, 'well?'

The older man had put his pistol back into the
breast of his brown coat.

'This is Lucien Lesage,' said he.

The hussar looked with disgust at the prostrate
figure upon the floor.

'A pretty conspirator!' said he. 'Get up, you
grovelling hound! Here, Gérard, take charge of
him and bring him into camp.'

A younger officer with two troopers at his heels
came clanking in to the hut, and the wretched
creature, half swooning, was dragged out into the
darkness.

'Where is the other — the man called
Toussac?'

'He killed the hound and escaped. Lesage
would have got away also had I not prevented
him. If you had kept the dog in leash we

"BUT WHO IS THIS?" ASKED GENERAL SAVARY, POINTING AT ME

should have had them both, but as it is, Colonel Lasalle, I think that you may congratulate me.' He held out his hand as he spoke, but the other turned abruptly on his heel.

' You hear that, General Savary?' said he, looking out of the door. ' Toussac has escaped.'

A tall, dark young man appeared within the circle of light cast by the lamp. The agitation of his handsome swarthy face showed the effect which the news had upon him.

' Where is he then?'

' It is a quarter of an hour since he got away.'

' But he is the only dangerous man of them all. The Emperor will be furious. In which direction did he fly?'

' It must have been inland.'

' But who is this?' asked General Savary, pointing at me. ' I understood from your information that there were only two besides yourself, Monsieur——.'

' I had rather no names were mentioned,' said the other abruptly.

' I can well understand that,' General Savary answered with a sneer.

'I would have told you that the cottage was the rendezvous, but it was not decided upon until the last moment. I gave you the means of tracking Toussac, but you let the hound slip. I certainly think that you will have to answer to the Emperor for the way in which you have managed the business.'

'That, sir, is our affair,' said General Savary sternly. 'In the meantime you have not told us who this person is.'

It seemed useless for me to conceal my identity, since I had a letter in my pocket which would reveal it.

'My name is Louis de Laval,' said I proudly.

I may confess that I think we had exaggerated our own importance over in England. We had thought that all France was wondering whether we should return, whereas in the quick march of events France had really almost forgotten our existence. This young General Savary was not in the least impressed by my aristocratic name, but he jotted it down in his notebook.

'Monsieur de Laval has nothing whatever to do with the matter,' said the spy. 'He has blundered into it entirely by chance, and I will answer for his safe keeping in case he should be wanted.'

'He will certainly be wanted,' said General Savary. 'In the meantime I need every trooper that I have for the chase, so, if you make yourself personally responsible, and bring him to the camp when needed, I see no objection to his remaining in your keeping. I shall send to you if I require him.'

'He will be at the Emperor's orders.'

'Are there any papers in the cottage?'

'They have been burned.'

'That is unfortunate.'

'But I have duplicates.'

'Excellent ! Come, Lasalle, every minute counts, and there is nothing to be done here. Let the men scatter, and we may still ride him down.'

The two tall soldiers clanked out of the cottage without taking any further notice of my companion, and I heard the sharp stern order and the jingling of metal as the troopers sprang back into their saddles once more. An instant later they were off, and I listened to the dull beat of their hoofs dying rapidly into a confused murmur. My little snuff-coloured champion went to the door of the hut and peered after them through the darkness. Then he came back and looked me up and down, with his usual dry sardonic smile.

'Well, young man,' said he, 'we have played some pretty *tableaux vivants* for your amusement, and you can thank me for that nice seat in the front row of the parterre.'

'I am under a very deep obligation to you, sir,' I answered, struggling between my gratitude and my aversion. 'I hardly know how to thank you.'

He looked at me with a singular expression in his ironical eyes.

'You will have the opportunity for thanking me later,' said he. 'In the meantime, as you say that you are a stranger upon our coast, and as I am responsible for your safe keeping, you cannot do better than follow me, and I will take you to a place where you may sleep in safety.'

CHAPTER VI

THE SECRET PASSAGE

THE fire had already smouldered down, and my companion blew out the lamp, so that we had not taken ten paces before we had lost sight of the ill-omened cottage, in which I had received so singular a welcome upon my home-coming. The wind had softened down, but a fine rain, cold and clammy, came drifting up from the sea. Had I been left to myself I should have found myself as much at a loss as I had been when I first landed; but my companion walked with a brisk and assured step, so that it was evident that he guided himself by landmarks which were invisible to me. For my part, wet and miserable, with my forlorn bundle under my arm, and my nerves all jangled by my terrible experiences, I trudged in silence by his side, turning over in my mind all that had occurred to me.

Young as I was, I had heard much political
discussion amongst my elders in England, and the
state of affairs in France was perfectly familiar to
me. I was aware that the recent elevation of
Buonaparte to the throne had enraged the small
but formidable section of Jacobins and extreme
Republicans, who saw that all their efforts to
abolish a kingdom had only ended in transforming
it into an empire. It was, indeed, a pitiable result
of their frenzied strivings that a crown with eight
fleurs-de-lis should be changed into a higher crown
surmounted by a cross and ball. On the other
hand, the followers of the Bourbons, in whose
company I had spent my youth, were equally dis-
appointed at the manner in which the mass of the
French people hailed this final step in the return
from chaos to order. Contradictory as were their
motives, the more violent spirits of both parties
were united in their hatred to Napoleon, and in
their fierce determination to get rid of him by
any means. Hence a series of conspiracies, most
of them with their base in England; and hence
also a large use of spies and informers upon the
part of Fouché and of Savary, upon whom the

responsibility of the safety of the Emperor lay. A strange chance had landed me upon the French coast at the very same time as a murderous conspirator, and had afterwards enabled me to see the weapons with which the police contrived to thwart and outwit him and his associates. When I looked back upon my series of adventures, my wanderings in the salt-marsh, my entrance into the cottage, my discovery of the papers, my capture by the conspirators, the long period of suspense with Toussac's dreadful thumb upon my chin, and finally the moving scenes which I had witnessed— the killing of the hound, the capture of Lesage, and the arrival of the soldiers—I could not wonder that my nerves were overwrought, and that I surprised myself in little convulsive gestures, like those of a frightened child.

The chief thought which now filled my mind was what my relations were with this dangerous man who walked by my side. His conduct and bearing had filled me with abhorrence. I had seen the depth of cunning with which he had duped and betrayed his companions, and I had read in his lean smiling face the cold deliberate cruelty of

his nature, as he stood, pistol in hand, over the
whimpering coward whom he had outwitted. Yet
I could not deny that when, through my own
foolish curiosity, I had placed myself in a most
hopeless position, it was he who had braved the
wrath of the formidable Toussac in order to extri-
cate me. It was evident also that he might have
made his achievement more striking by delivering
up two prisoners instead of one to the troopers.
It is true that I was not a conspirator, but I might
have found it difficult to prove it. So inconsistent
did such conduct seem in this little yellow flint-
stone of a man that, after walking a mile or two in
silence, I asked him suddenly what the meaning
of it might be.

I heard a dry chuckle in the darkness, as if he
were amused by the abruptness and directness of
my question.

'You are a most amusing person, Monsieur—
Monsieur—let me see, what did you say your name
was?'

'De Laval.'

'Ah, quite so, Monsieur de Laval. You have
the impetuosity and the ingenuousness of youth.

You want to know what is up a chimney, you jump
up the chimney. You want to know the reason of
a thing, and you blurt out a question. I have
been in the habit of living among people who keep
their thoughts to themselves, and I find you very
refreshing.'

'Whatever the motives of your conduct, there
is no doubt that you saved my life,' said I. 'I am
much obliged to you for your intercession.' It is
the most difficult thing in the world to express
gratitude to a person who fills you with abhorrence,
and I fear that my halting speech was another
instance of that ingenuousness of which he accused
me.

'I can do without your thanks,' said he coldly.
' You are perfectly right when you think that if it
had suited my purpose I should have let you perish,
and I am perfectly right when I think that if it
were not that you are under an obligation you
would fail to see my hand if I stretched it out to
you just as that overgrown puppy Lasalle did. It
is very honourable, he thinks, to serve the Emperor
upon the field of battle, and to risk life in his
behalf, but when it comes to living amidst danger

G

as I have done, consorting with desperate men, and knowing well that the least slip would mean death, why then one is beneath the notice of a fine clean-handed gentleman. Why,' he continued in a burst of bitter passion, ' I have dared more, and endured more, with Toussac and a few of his kidney for comrades, than this Lasalle has done in all the childish cavalry charges that ever he under-took. As to service, all his Marshals put together have not rendered the Emperor as pressing a service as I have done. But I daresay it does not strike you in that light, Monsieur—Monsieur——'

' De Laval.'

' Quite so—it is curious how that name escapes me. I daresay you take the same view as Colonel Lasalle ? '

' It is not a question upon which I can offer an opinion,' said I. ' I only know that I owe my life to your intercession.'

I do not know what reply he might have made to this evasion, but at that moment we heard a couple of pistol shots and a distant shouting from far away in the darkness. We stopped for a few minutes, but all was silent once more.

'They must have caught sight of Toussac,' said my companion. 'I am afraid that he is too strong and too cunning to be taken by them. I do not know what impression he left upon you, but I can tell you that you will go far to meet a more dangerous man.'

I answered that I would go far to avoid meeting one, unless I had the means of defending myself, and my companion's dry chuckle showed that he appreciated my feelings.

'Yet he is an absolutely honest man, which is no very common thing in these days,' said he. 'He is one of those who, at the outbreak of the Revolution, embraced it with the whole strength of his simple nature. He believed what the writers and the speakers told him, and he was convinced that, after a little disturbance and a few necessary executions, France was to become a heaven upon earth, the centre of peace and comfort and brotherly love. A good many people got those fine ideas into their heads, but the heads have mostly dropped into the sawdust-basket by this time. Toussac was true to them, and when instead of peace he found war, instead of comfort a grinding poverty,

and instead of equality an Empire, it drove him
mad. He became the fierce creature you see, with
the one idea of devoting his huge body and giant's
strength to the destruction of those who had interfered with his ideal. He is fearless, persevering,
and implacable. I have no doubt at all that he
will kill me for the part that I have played
to-night.'

It was in the calmest voice that my companion
uttered the remark, and it made me understand
that it was no boast when he said there was more
courage needed to carry on his unsavoury trade
than to play the part of a *beau sabreur* like Lasalle.
He paused a little, and then went on as if speaking
to himself.

'Yes,' said he, 'I missed my chance. I certainly
ought to have shot him when he was struggling
with the hound. But if I had only wounded him
he would have torn me into bits like an over-boiled
pullet, so perhaps it is as well as it is.'

We had left the salt-marsh behind us, and for
some time I had felt the soft springy turf of the
downland beneath my feet, and our path had risen
and dipped over the curves of the low coast hills.

In spite of the darkness my companion walked with
great assurance, never hesitating for an instant, and
keeping up a stiff pace which was welcome to me
in my sodden and benumbed condition. I had
been so young when I left my native place that it
is doubtful whether, even in daylight, I should have
recognised the countryside, but now in the darkness, half stupefied by my adventures, I could not
form the least idea as to where we were or what we
were making for. A certain recklessness had taken
possession of me, and I cared little where I went as
long as I could gain the rest and shelter of which
I stood in need.

I do not know how long we had walked; I only
know that I had dozed and woke and dozed again
whilst still automatically keeping pace with my
comrade, when I was at last aroused by his coming
to a dead stop. The rain had ceased, and although
the moon was still obscured, the heavens had cleared
somewhat, and I could see for a little distance in
every direction. A huge white basin gaped in front
of us, and I made out that it was a deserted chalk
quarry, with brambles and ferns growing thickly
all round the edges. My companion, after a stealthy

glance round to make sure that no one was observing us, picked his way amongst the scattered clumps of bushes until he reached the wall of chalk. This he skirted for some distance, squeezing between the cliff and the brambles until he came at last to a spot where all further progress appeared to be impossible.

'Can you see a light behind us?' asked my companion.

I turned round and looked carefully in every direction, but was unable to see one.

'Never mind,' said he. 'You go first, and I will follow.'

In some way during the instant that my back had been turned he had swung aside or plucked out the tangle of bush which had barred our way. When I turned there was a square dark opening in the white glimmering wall in front of us.

'It is small at the entrance, but it grows larger further in,' said he.

I hesitated for an instant. Whither was it that this strange man was leading me? Did he live in a cave like a wild beast, or was this some trap into which he was luring me? The moon shone out at the instant, and in its silver light this black, silent porthole looked inexpressibly cheerless and menacing.

'You have gone rather far to turn back, my good friend,' said my companion. 'You must either trust me altogether or not trust me at all.'

'I am at your disposal.'

'Pass in then, and I shall follow.'

I crept into the narrow passage, which was so low that I had to crawl down it upon my hands and knees. Craning my neck round, I could see the black angular silhouette of my companion as he came after me. He paused at the entrance, and then, with a rustling of branches and snapping of twigs, the faint light was suddenly shut off from outside, and we were left in pitchy darkness. I heard the scraping of his knees as he crawled up behind me.

'Go on until you come to a step down,' said he. 'We shall have more room there, and we can strike a light.'

The ceiling was so low that by arching my back I could easily strike it, and my elbows touched the wall upon either side. In those days I was slim and lithe, however, so that I found no difficulty in making my way onwards until, at the end of a hundred paces, or it may have been a hundred and fifty, I felt with my hands that there was a dip in front of me. Down this I clambered, and was instantly conscious from the purer air that I was in some larger cavity. I heard the snapping of my companion's flint, and the red glow of the tinder paper leaped suddenly into the clear yellow flame of the taper. At first I could only see that stern, emaciated face, like some grotesque carving in walnut wood, with the ceaseless fishlike vibration of the muscles of his jaw. The light beat full upon it, and it stood strangely out with a dim halo round it in the darkness. Then he raised the taper and swept it slowly round at arm's length so as to illuminate the place in which we stood.

I found that we were in a subterranean tunnel, which appeared to extend into the bowels of the earth. It was so high that I could stand erect with ease, and the old lichen-blotched stones which lined the walls told of its great age. At the spot where we stood the ceiling had fallen in and the original passage been blocked, but a cutting had been made from this point through the chalk to form the narrow burrow along which we had come. This cutting appeared to be quite recent, for a mound of *débris* and some trenching tools were still lying in the passage. My companion, taper in hand, started off down the tunnel, and I followed at his heels, stepping over the great stones which had fallen from the roof or the walls, and now obstructed the path.

' Well,' said he, grinning at me over his shoulder, ' have you ever seen anything like this in England ? '

' Never,' I answered.

' These are the precautions and devices which men adopted in rough days long ago. Now that rough days have come again, they are very useful to those who know of such places.'

' Whither does it lead, then ? ' I asked.

' To this,' said he, stopping before an old wooden door, powerfully clamped with iron. He fumbled with the metal-work, keeping himself between me and it, so that I could not see what he was doing. There was a sharp snick, and the door revolved slowly upon its hinges. Within there was a steep flight of time-worn steps leading upwards. He

motioned me on, and closed the door behind us.
At the head of the stair there was a second wooden
gate, which he opened in a similar manner.

I had been dazed before ever I came into the
chalk pit, but now, at this succession of incidents,
I began to rub my eyes and ask myself whether
this was young Louis de Laval, late of Ashford, in
Kent, or whether it was some dream of the adventures of a hero of Pigault Lebrun. These massive
moss-grown arches and mighty iron-clamped doors
were, indeed, like the dim shadowy background of
a vision; but the guttering taper, my sodden
bundle, and all the sordid details of my disarranged
toilet assured me only too clearly of their reality.
Above all, the swift, brisk, business-like manner of
my companion, and his occasional abrupt remarks,
brought my fancies back to the ground once more.
He held the door open for me now, and closed it
again when I had passed through.

We found ourselves in a long vaulted corridor,
with a stone-flagged floor, and a dim oil lamp burning at the further end. Two iron-barred windows
showed that we had come above the earth's surface
once more. Down this corridor we passed, and

then through several passages and up a short winding stair. At the head of it was an open door, which led into a small but comfortable bedroom.

'I presume that this will satisfy your wants for to-night,' said he.

I asked for nothing better than to throw myself down, damp clothes and all, upon that snowy coverlet; but for the instant my curiosity overcame my fatigue.

'I am much indebted to you, sir,' said I. 'Perhaps you will add to your favours by letting me know where I am.'

'You are in my house, and that must suffice you for to-night. In the morning we shall go further into the matter.' He rang a small bell, and a gaunt shock-headed country man-servant came running at the call.

'Your mistress has retired, I suppose?'

'Yes, sir, a good two hours ago.'

'Very good. I shall call you myself in the morning.' He closed my door, and the echo of his steps seemed hardly to have died from my ears before I had sunk into that deep and dreamless sleep which only youth and fatigue can give.

CHAPTER VII

THE OWNER OF GROSBOIS

My host was as good as his word, for, when a noise in my room awoke me in the morning, it was to find him standing by the side of my bed, so composed in his features and so drab in his attire, that it was hard to associate him with the stirring scenes of yesterday and with the repulsive part which he had played in them. Now in the fresh morning sunlight he presented rather the appearance of a pedantic schoolmaster, an impression which was increased by the masterful, and yet benevolent, smile with which he regarded me. In spite of his smile, I was more conscious than ever that my whole soul shrank from him, and that I should not be at my ease until I had broken this companionship which had been so involuntarily formed. He carried a heap of clothes over one arm, which he threw upon a chair at the bottom of my bed.

'I gather from the little that you told me last night,' said he, 'that your wardrobe is at present somewhat scanty. I fear that your inches are greater than those of anyone in my household, but I have brought a few things here amongst which you may find something to fit you. Here, too, are the razors, the soap, and the powder-box. I will return in half an hour, when your toilet will doubtless be completed.'

I found that my own clothes, with a little brushing, were as good as ever, but I availed myself of his offer to the extent of a ruffled shirt and a black satin cravat. I had finished dressing and was looking out of the window of my room, which opened on to a blank wall, when my host returned. He looked me all over with a keenly scrutinising eye, and appeared to be satisfied with what he saw.

'That will do! That will do very well indeed!' said he, nodding a critical head. 'In these times a slight indication of travel or hard work upon a costume is more fashionable than the foppishness of the Incroyable. I have heard ladies remark that it was in better taste. Now, sir, if you will kindly follow me.

His solicitude about my dress filled me with surprise, but this was soon forgotten in the shock which was awaiting me. For as we passed down the passage and into a large hall which seemed strangely familiar to me, there was a full-length portrait of my father standing right in front of me. I stood staring with a gasp of astonishment, and turned to see the cold grey eyes of my companion fixed upon me with a humorous glitter.

'You seem surprised, Monsieur de Laval,' said he.

'For God's sake,' said I, 'do not trifle with me any further! Who are you, and what is this place to which you have taken me?'

For answer he broke into one of his dry chuckles, and, laying his skinny brown hand upon my wrist, he led me into a large apartment. In the centre was a table, tastefully laid, and beyond it in a low chair a young lady was seated, with a book in her hand. She rose as we entered, and I saw that she was tall and slender, with a dark face, pronounced features, and black eyes of extraordinary brilliancy. Even in that one glance it struck me that the expression with which she regarded me was by no means a friendly one.

SHE ROSE AS WE ENTERED, AND I SAW THAT SHE WAS TALL AND SLENDER

'Sibylle,' said my host, and his words took the breath from my lips, 'this is your cousin from England, Louis de Laval. This, my dear nephew, is my only daughter, Sibylle Bernac.'

'Then you——'

'I am your mother's brother, Charles Bernac.'

'You are my Uncle Bernac !' I stammered at him like an idiot. 'But why did you not tell me so ?' I cried.

'I was not sorry to have a chance of quietly observing what his English education had done for my nephew. It might also have been harder for me to stand your friend if my comrades had any reason to think that I was personally interested in you. But you will permit me now to welcome you heartily to France, and to express my regret if your reception has been a rough one. I am sure that Sibylle will help me to atone for it. He smiled archly at his daughter, who continued to regard me with a stony face.

I looked round me, and gradually the spacious room, with the weapons upon the wall, and the deer's heads, came dimly back to my memory. That view through the oriel window, too, with the

clump of oaks in the sloping park, and the sea in
the distance beyond, I had certainly seen it before.
It was true then, and I was in our own castle of
Grosbois, and this dreadful man in the snuff-
coloured coat, this sinister plotter with the death's-
head face, was the man whom I had heard my
poor father curse so often, the man who had ousted
him from his own property and installed himself in
his place. And yet I could not forget that it was
he also who, at some risk to himself, had saved me
the night before, and my soul was again torn
between my gratitude and my repulsion.

We had seated ourselves at the table, and as
we ate, this newly-found uncle of mine continued
to explain all those points which I had failed to
understand.

'I suspected that it was you the instant that I
set eyes upon you,' said he. 'I am old enough to
remember your father when he was a young gallant,
and you are his very double—though I may say,
without flattery, that where there is a difference it
is in your favour. And yet he had the name of
being one of the handsomest men betwixt Rouen
and the sea. You must bear in mind that I was

expecting you, and that there are not so many
young aristocrats of your age wandering about
along the coast. I was surprised when you did not
recognise where you were last night. Had you
never heard of the secret passage of Grosbois ? '

It came vaguely back to me that in my childhood I had heard of this underground tunnel, but
that the roof had fallen in and rendered it useless.

'Precisely,' said my uncle. ' When the castle
passed into my hands, one of the very first things
which I did was to cut a new opening at the end of
it, for I foresaw that in these troublesome times
it might be of use to me ; indeed, had it been in
repair it might have made the escape of your
mother and father a very much easier affair.'

His words recalled all that I had heard and all
that I could remember of those dreadful days when
we, the Lords of the country side, had been chased
across it as if we had been wolves, with the howling mob still clustering at the pier-head to shake
their fists and hurl their stones at us. I remembered, too, that it was this very man who
was speaking to me who had thrown oil upon the
flames in those days, and whose fortunes had been

H

founded upon our ruin.   As I looked across at him
I found that his keen grey eyes were fixed upon
me, and I could see that he had read the thoughts
in my mind.

'We must let bygones be bygones,' said he.
'Those are quarrels of the last generation, and
Sibylle and you represent a new one.'

My cousin had not said one word or taken any
notice of my presence, but at this joining of our
names she glanced at me with the same hostile
expression which I had already remarked.

'Come, Sibylle,' said her father, 'you can assure
your cousin Louis that, so far as you are concerned, any family misunderstanding is at an end.'

'It is very well for us to talk in that way,
father,' she answered.   'It is not your picture that
hangs in the hall, or your coat-of-arms that I see
upon the wall.   We hold the castle and the land,
but it is for the heir of the de Lavals to tell us if
he is satisfied with this.'   Her dark scornful eyes
were fixed upon me as she waited for my reply,
but her father hastened to intervene.

'This is not a very hospitable tone in which
to greet your cousin,' said he harshly.   'It has so

chanced that Louis' heritage has fallen to us, but it is not for us to remind him of the fact.'

'He needs no reminding,' said she.

'You do me an injustice,' I cried, for the evident and malignant scorn of this girl galled me to the quick. 'It is true that I cannot forget that this castle and these grounds belonged to my ancestors—I should be a clod indeed if I *could* forget it—but if you think that I harbour any bitterness, you are mistaken. For my own part, I ask nothing better than to open up a career for myself with my own sword.'

'And never was there a time when it could be more easily and more brilliantly done,' cried my uncle. 'There are great things about to happen in the world, and if you are at the Emperor's court you will be in the middle of them. I understand that you are content to serve him ?

'I wish to serve my country.'

'By serving the Emperor you do so, for without him the country becomes chaos.'

'From all we hear it is not a very easy service,' said my cousin. 'I should have thought that you would have been very much more comfortable in

England—and then you would have been so much
safer also.'

Everything which the girl said seemed to be
meant as an insult to me, and yet I could not
imagine how I had ever offended her. Never had
I met a woman for whom I conceived so hearty
and rapid a dislike. I could see that her remarks
were as offensive to her father as they were to me,
for he looked at her with eyes which were as angry
as her own.

'Your cousin is a brave man, and that is more
than can be said for someone else that I could
mention,' said he.

'For whom?' she asked.

'Never mind!' he snapped, and, jumping up
with the air of a man who is afraid that his rage
may master him, and that he may say more than
he wished, he ran from the room.

She seemed startled by this retort of his, and
rose as if she would follow him. Then she tossed
her head and laughed incredulously.

'I suppose that you have never met your uncle
before?' said she, after a few minutes of embar-
rassed silence.

'Never,' answered I.

'Well, what do you think of him now you *have* met him ?'

Such a question from a daughter about her father filled me with a certain vague horror. I felt that he must be even a worse man than I had taken him for if he had so completely forfeited the loyalty of his own nearest and dearest.

'Your silence is a sufficient answer,' said she, as I hesitated for a reply. 'I do not know how you came to meet him last night, or what passed between you, for we do not share each other's confidences. I think, however, that you have read him aright. Now I have something to ask you. You had a letter from him inviting you to leave England and to come here, had you not ?'

'Yes, I had.'

'Did you observe nothing on the outside ?'

I thought of those two sinister words which had puzzled me so much.

'What ! it was you who warned me not to come ?'

'Yes, it was I. I had no other means of doing it.'

' But why did you do it ? '

' Because I did not wish you to come here.'

' Did you think that I would harm you ? '

She sat silent for a few seconds like one who is afraid of saying too much. When her answer came it was a very unexpected one :

' I was afraid that you would be harmed.'

' You think that I am in danger here ? '

' I am sure of it.'

' You advise me to leave ? '

' Without losing an instant.'

' From whom is the danger then ? '

Again she hesitated, and then, with a reckless motion like one who throws prudence to the winds, she turned upon me.

' It is from my father,' said she.

' But why should he harm me ? '

' That is for your sagacity to discover.'

' But I assure you, mademoiselle, that in this matter you misjudge him,' said I. ' As it happens, he interfered to save my life last night.'

' To save your life ! From whom ? '

' From two conspirators whose plans I had chanced to discover.'

'Conspirators!' She looked at me in surprise. 'They would have killed me if he had 'not intervened.'

'It is not his interest that you should be harmed yet awhile. He had reasons for wishing you to come to Castle Grosbois. But I have been very frank with you, and I wish you to be equally so with me. Does it happen—does it happen that during your youth in England you have ever—you have ever had an affair of the heart?'

Everything which this cousin of mine said appeared to me to be stranger than the last, and this question, coming at the end of so serious a conversation, was the strangest of all. But frankness begets frankness, and I did not hesitate.

'I have left the very best and truest girl in the world behind me in England,' said I. 'Eugénie is her name, Eugénie de Choiseul, the niece of the old Duke.'

My reply seemed to give my cousin great satisfaction. Her large dark eyes shone with pleasure.

'You are very attached?' she asked.

'I shall never be happy until I see her.'

'And you would not give her up?'

'God forbid!'

'Not for the Castle of Grosbois?'

'Not even for that.'

My cousin held out her hand to me with a charmingly frank impulsiveness.

'You will forgive me for my rudeness,' said she. 'I see that we are to be allies and not enemies.'

And our hands were still clasped when her father re-entered the room.

CHAPTER VIII

COUSIN SIBYLLE

I COULD see in my uncle's grim face as he looked at us the keenest satisfaction contending with surprise at this sign of our sudden reconciliation. All trace of his recent anger seemed to have left him as he addressed his daughter, but in spite of his altered tone I noticed that her eyes looked defiance and distrust.

' I have some papers of importance to look over,' said he. ' For an hour or so I shall be engaged. I can guess that Louis would like to see the old place once again, and I am sure that he could not have a better guide than you, Sibylle, if you will take him over it.'

She raised no objection, and for my part I was overjoyed at the proposal, as it gave me an opportunity of learning more of this singular cousin of mine, who had told me so much and yet seemed to

know so much more. What was the meaning of
this obscure warning which she had given me
against her father, and why was she so frankly
anxious to know about my love affairs ? These were
the two questions which pressed for an answer. So
out we went together into the sweet coast-land air,
the sweeter for the gale of the night before, and we
walked through the old yew-lined paths, and out
into the park, and so round the castle, looking up
at the gables, the grey pinnacles, the oak-mullioned
windows, the ancient wing with its crenulated walls
and its meurtrière windows, the modern with its
pleasant verandah and veil of honeysuckle. And
as she showed me each fresh little detail, with a
particularity which made me understand how dear
the place had become to her, she would still keep
offering her apologies for the fact that she should
be the hostess and I the visitor.

'It is not against you but against ourselves that
I was bitter,' said she, 'for are we not the cuckoos
who have taken a strange nest and driven out those
who built it ? It makes me blush to think that my
father should invite you to your own house.'

'Perhaps we had been rooted here too long,' I

answered. 'Perhaps it is for our own good that we are driven out to carve our own fortunes, as I intend to do.'

'You say that you are going to the Emperor ?'

'Yes.'

'You know that he is in camp near here ?'

'So I have heard.'

'But your family is still proscribed ?'

'I have done him no harm. I will go bold to him and ask him to admit me into his service.'

'Well,' said she, 'there are some who call him a usurper, and wish him all evil; but for my own part I have never heard of anything that he has said and done which was not great and noble. But I had expected that you would be quite an Englishman, Cousin Louis, and come over here with your pockets full of Pitt's guineas and your heart of treason.'

'I have met nothing but hospitality from the English,' I answered; 'but my heart has always been French.'

'But your father fought against us at Quiberon.'

'Let each generation settle its own quarrels,'

said I. 'I am quite of your father's opinion about
that.'

'Do not judge my father by his words, but by his
deeds,' said she, with a warning finger upraised ;
'and, above all, Cousin Louis, unless you wish to
have my life upon your conscience, never let him
suspect that I have said a word to set you on your
guard.'

'Your life !' I gasped.

'Oh, yes, he would not stick at that !' she cried.
'He killed my mother. I do not say that he
slaughtered her, but I mean that his cold brutality
broke her gentle heart. Now perhaps you begin
to understand why I can talk of him in this
fashion.'

As she spoke I could see the secret broodings
of years, the bitter resentments crushed down in
her silent soul, rising suddenly to flush her dark
cheeks and to gleam in her splendid eyes. I
realised at that moment that in that tall slim
figure there dwelt an unconquerable spirit.

'You must think that I speak very freely to
you, since I have only known you a few hours,
Cousin Louis,' said she.

'To whom should you speak freely if not to your own relative?'

'It is true; and yet I never expected that I should be on such terms with you. I looked forward to your coming with dread and sorrow. No doubt I showed something of my feelings when my father brought you in.'

'Indeed you did,' I answered. 'I feared that my presence was unwelcome to you.'

'Most unwelcome, both for your own sake and for mine,' said she. 'For your sake because I suspected, as I have told you, that my father's intentions might be unfriendly. For mine——'

'Why for yours?' I asked in surprise, for she had stopped in embarrassment.

'You have told me that your heart is another's. I may tell you that my hand is also promised, and that my love has gone with it.'

'May all happiness attend it!' said I. 'But why should this make my coming unwelcome?'

'That thick English air has dimmed your wits, cousin,' said she, shaking her stately head at me. 'But I can speak freely now that I know that this plan would be as hateful to you as to me. You

must know, then, that if my father could have
married us he would have united all claims to the
succession of Grosbois.   Then, come what might—
Bourbon or Buonaparte—nothing could shake his
position.'

I thought of the solicitude which he had shown
over my toilet in the morning, his anxiety that
I should make a favourable impression, his dis-
pleasure when she had been cold to me, and the
smile upon his face when he had seen us hand in
hand.

'I believe you are right!' I cried.

'Right!   Of course I am right!   Look at him
watching us now.'

We were walking on the edge of the dried moat,
and as I looked up there, sure enough, was the
little yellow face turned towards us in the angle of
one of the windows.   Seeing that I was watching
him, he rose and waved his hand merrily.

'Now you know why he saved your life—since
you say that he saved it,' said she.   'It would
suit his plans best that you should marry his
daughter, and so he wished you to live.   But when
once he understands that that is impossible, why

then, my poor Cousin Louis, his only way of
guarding against the return of the de Lavals must
lie in ensuring that there are none to return.'

It was those words of hers, coupled with that
furtive yellow face still lurking at the window,
which made me realise the imminence of my
danger. No one in France had any reason to
take an interest in me. If I were to pass away
there was no one who could make inquiry—I was
absolutely in his power. My memory told me
what a ruthless and dangerous man it was with
whom I had to deal.

'But,' said I, 'he must have known that your
affections were already engaged.'

'He did,' she answered; 'it was that which
made me most uneasy of all. I was afraid for you
and afraid for myself, but, most of all, I was
afraid for Lucien. No man can stand in the way
of his plans.'

'Lucien!' The name was like a lightning flash
upon a dark night. I had heard of the vagaries
of a woman's love, but was it possible that this
spirited woman loved that poor creature whom I
had seen grovelling last night in a frenzy of fear?

But now I remembered also where I had seen the
name Sibylle. It was upon the fly-leaf of his
book. 'Lucien, from Sibylle,' was the inscription.
I recalled also that my uncle had said something
to him about his aspirations.

'Lucien is hot-headed, and easily carried away,'
said she. 'My father has seen a great deal of
him lately. They sit for hours in his room, and
Lucien will say nothing of what passes between
them. I fear that there is something going
forward which may lead to evil. Lucien is a
student rather than a man of the world, but he
has strong opinions about politics.'

I was at my wit's ends what to do, whether to
be silent, or to tell her of the terrible position in
which her lover was placed; but, even as I hesitated, she, with the quick intuition of a woman,
read the doubts which were in my mind.

'You know something of him,' she cried. 'I
understood that he had gone to Paris. For God's
sake tell me what you know about him!'

'His name is Lesage?'

'Yes, yes. Lucien Lesage.'

'I have—I have seen him,' I stammered.

SHE GRIPPED ME BY THE WRIST IN HER ANXIETY

'You have seen him! And you only arrived in France last night. Where did you see him? What has happened to him?' She gripped me by the wrist in her anxiety.

It was cruel to tell her, and yet it seemed more cruel still to keep silent. I looked round in my bewilderment, and there was my uncle himself coming along over the close-cropped green lawn. By his side, with a merry clashing of steel and jingling of spurs, there walked a handsome young hussar—the same to whom the charge of the prisoner had been committed upon the night before. Sibylle never hesitated for an instant, but, with a set face and blazing eyes, she swept towards them.

'Father,' said she, 'what have you done with Lucien?'

I saw his impassive face wince for a moment before the passionate hatred and contempt which he read in her eyes. 'We will discuss this at some future time,' said he.

'I will know here and now,' she cried. 'What have you done with Lucien?'

'Gentlemen,' said he, turning to the young

I

hussar and me, 'I am sorry that we should intrude our little domestic differences upon your attention. You will, I am sure, make allowances, lieutenant, when I tell you that your prisoner of last night was a very dear friend of my daughter's. Such family considerations do not prevent me from doing my duty to the Emperor, but they make that duty more painful than it would otherwise be.'

'You have my sympathy, mademoiselle,' said the young hussar.

It was to him that my cousin had now turned.

'Do I understand that you took him prisoner?' she asked.

'It was unfortunately my duty.'

'From you I will get the truth. Whither did you take him?'

'To the Emperor's camp.'

'And why?'

'Ah, mademoiselle, it is not for me to go into politics. My duties are but to wield a sword, and sit a horse, and obey my orders. Both these gentlemen will be my witnesses that I received my instructions from Colonel Lasalle.'

'But on what charge was he arrested?'

'Tut, tut, child, we have had enough of this!' said my uncle harshly. 'If you insist upon knowing I will tell you once and for all, that Monsieur Lucien Lesage has been seized for being concerned in a plot against the life of the Emperor, and that it was my privilege to denounce the would-be assassin.'

'To denounce him!' cried the girl. 'I know that it was you who set him on, who encouraged him, who held him to it whenever he tried to draw back. Oh, you villain! you villain! What have I ever done, what sin of my ancestors am I expiating, that I should be compelled to call such a man Father?'

My uncle shrugged his shoulders as if to say that it was useless to argue with a woman's tantrums. The hussar and I made as if we would stroll away, for it was embarrassing to stand listening to such words, but in her fury she called to us to stop and be witnesses against him. Never have I seen such a recklessness of passion as blazed in her dry wide-opened eyes.

'You have deceived others, but you have never deceived me,' she cried. 'I know you as your own conscience knows you. You may murder me, as you murdered my mother before me, but you can never frighten me into being your accomplice. You proclaimed yourself a Republican that you might creep into a house and estate which do not belong to you. And now you try to make a friend of Buonaparte by betraying your old associates, who still trust in you. And you have sent Lucien to his death! But I know your plans, and my Cousin Louis knows them also, and I can assure you that there is just as much chance of his agreeing to them as there is of my doing so. I'd rather lie in my grave than be the wife of any man but Lucien.'

'If you had seen the pitiful poltroon that he proved himself you would not say so,' said my uncle coolly. 'You are not yourself at present, but when you return to your right mind you will be ashamed of having made this public exposure of your weakness. And now, lieutenant, you have something to say.'

'My message was to you, Monsieur de Laval,' said the young hussar, turning his back contemptuously upon my uncle. 'The Emperor has sent me to bring you to him at once at the camp at Boulogne.'

My heart leapt at the thought of escaping from my uncle.

'I ask nothing better,' I cried.

'A horse and an escort are waiting at the gates.'

'I am ready to start at this instant.'

'Nay, there can be no such very great hurry,' said my uncle. 'Surely you will wait for luncheon, Lieutenant Gérard.'

'The Emperor's commissions, sir, are not carried out in such a manner,' said the young hussar sternly. 'I have already wasted too much time. We must be upon our way in five minutes.'

My uncle placed his hand upon my arm and led me slowly towards the gateway, through which my cousin Sibylle had already passed.

'There is one matter that I wish to speak to you about before you go. Since my time is so short you will forgive me if I introduce it without preamble. You have seen your cousin Sibylle, and though her behaviour this morning is such as to prejudice you against her, yet I can assure you that she is a very amiable girl. She spoke just now as if she had mentioned the plan which I had conceived to you. I confess to you that I cannot imagine anything more convenient than that we should unite in order to settle once for all every question as to which branch of the family shall hold the estates.'

'Unfortunately,' said I, 'there are objections.'

'And pray what are they?'

'The fact that my cousin's hand, as I have just learned, is promised to another.'

'That need not hinder us,' said he, with a sour smile; 'I will undertake that he never claims the promise.'

'I fear that I have the English idea of marriage, that it should go by love and not by convenience. But in any case your scheme is out of the question, for my own affections are pledged to a young lady in England.'

He looked wickedly at me out of the corners of his grey eyes.

'Think well what you are doing, Louis,' said he, in a sibilant whisper which was as menacing as a serpent's hiss. 'You are deranging my plans, and that is not done with impunity.'

'It is not a matter in which I have any choice.'

He gripped me by the sleeve, and waved his hand round as Satan may have done when he showed the kingdoms and principalities. 'Look at the park,' he cried, 'the fields, the woods. Look at the old castle in which your fathers have lived for eight hundred years. You have but to say the word and it is all yours once more.'

There flashed up into my memory the little red-brick house at Ashford, and Eugénie's sweet pale face looking over the laurel bushes which grew by the window.

'It is impossible!' said I.

There must have been something in my manner which made him comprehend that it really was so, for his face darkened with anger, and his persuasion changed in an instant to menace.

'If I had known this they might have done what they wished with you last night,' said he. 'I would never have put out a finger to save you.'

'I am glad to hear you say so,' I answered, 'for it makes it easier for me to say that I wish to go my own way, and to have nothing more to do with you. What you have just said frees me from the bond of gratitude which held me back.'

'I have no doubt that you would like to have nothing more to do with me,' he cried. 'You will wish it more heartily still before you finish. Very well, sir, go your own way and I will go mine, and we shall see who comes out the best in the end.'

A group of hussars were standing by their horses' heads in the gateway. In a few minutes I had packed my scanty possessions, and I was hastening with them down the corridor when a chill struck suddenly through my heart at the thought of my cousin Sibylle. How could I leave her alone with this grim companion in the old castle? Had she not herself told me that her very life might be at stake? I had stopped in my perplexity, and suddenly there was a patter of feet, and there she was running towards me.

'Good-bye, Cousin Louis,' she cried, with outstretched hands.

'I was thinking of you,' said I; 'your father and I have had an explanation and a quarrel.'

'Thank God!' she cried. 'Your only chance was to get away from him. But beware, for he will do you an injury if he can!'

'He may do his worst; but how can I leave you here in his power?'

'Have no fears about me. He has more reason to avoid me than I him. But they are calling for you, Cousin Louis. Good-bye, and God be with you!'

CHAPTER IX

THE CAMP OF BOULOGNE

My uncle was still standing at the castle gateway, the very picture of a usurper, with our own old coat-of-arms of the bend argent and the three blue martlets engraved upon the stones at either side of him. He gave me no sign of greeting as I mounted the large grey horse which was awaiting me, but he looked thoughtfully at me from under his down-drawn brows, and his jaw muscles still throbbed with that stealthy rhythmical movement. I read a cold and settled malice in his set yellow face and his stern eyes. For my own part I sprang readily enough into the saddle, for the man's presence had, from the first, been loathsome to me, and I was right glad to be able to turn my back upon him. And so, with a stern quick order from the lieutenant and a jingle and clatter from the troopers, we were off upon our journey. As I

glanced back at the black keep of Grosbois, and at
the sinister figure who stood looking after us
from beside the gateway, I saw from over his head
a white handkerchief gleam for an instant in a last
greeting from one of the gloomy meurtrière windows,
and again a chill ran through me as I thought of
the fearless girl and of the hands in which we
were leaving her.

But sorrow clears from the mind of youth like
the tarnish of breath upon glass, and who could
carry a heavy heart upon so lightfooted a horse
and through so sweet an air ? The white glimmering road wound over the downs with the sea far
upon the left, and between lay that great salt-
marsh which had been the scene of our adventures.
I could even see, as I fancied, a dull black spot in
the distance to mark the position of that terrible
cottage. Far away the little clusters of houses
showed the positions of Etaples, Ambleterre, and
the other fishing villages, whilst I could see that
the point which had seemed last night to glow
like a half-forged red-hot sword-blade was now
white as a snow-field with the camp of a great
army. Far, far away, a little dim cloud upon

the water stood for the land where I had spent my days—the pleasant, homely land which will always rank next to my own in my affections.

And now I turned my attention from the downs and the sea to the hussars who rode beside me, forming, as I could perceive, a guard rather than an escort. Save for the patrol last night, they were the first of the famous soldiers of Napoleon whom I had ever seen, and it was with admiration and curiosity that I looked upon men who had won a world-wide reputation for their discipline and their gallantry. Their appearance was by no means gorgeous, and their dress and equipment was much more modest than that of the East Kent Yeomanry, which rode every Saturday through Ashford; but the stained tunics, the worn leathers, and the rough hardy horses gave them a very workmanlike appearance. They were small, light, brown-faced fellows, heavily whiskered and moustached, many of them wearing ear-rings in their ears. It surprised me that even the youngest and most boyish-looking of them should be so bristling with hair, until, upon a second look, I perceived that his whiskers were

formed of lumps of black wax stuck on to the
sides of his face.   The tall young lieutenant
noticed the astonishment with which I gazed at
his boyish trooper.

'Yes, yes,' said he, 'they are artificial, sure
enough; but what can you expect from a lad of
seventeen?   On the other hand, we cannot spoil
the appearance of the regiment upon parade by
having a girl's cheeks in the ranks.'

'It melts terribly in this warm weather, lieutenant,' said the hussar, joining in the conversation with the freedom which was one of the
characteristics of Napoleon's troops.

'Well, well, Caspar, in a year or two you will
dispense with them.'

'Who knows?   Perhaps he will have dispensed
with his head also by that time,' said a corporal in
front, and they all laughed together in a manner
which in England would have meant a court-martial.
This seemed to me to be one of the survivals of
the Revolution, that officer and private were left
upon a very familiar footing, which was increased,
no doubt, by the freedom with which the Emperor
would chat with his old soldiers, and the liberties

which he would allow them to take with him. It was no uncommon thing for a shower of chaff to come from the ranks directed at their own commanding officers, and I am sorry to say, also, that it was no very unusual thing for a shower of bullets to come also. Unpopular officers were continually assassinated by their own men; at the battle of Montebello it is well known that every officer, with the exception of one lieutenant belonging to the 24th demi-brigade, was shot down from behind. But this was a relic of the bad times, and, as the Emperor gained more complete control, a better feeling was established. The history of our army at that time proved, at any rate, that the highest efficiency could be maintained without the flogging which was still used in the Prussian and the English service, and it was shown, for the first time, that great bodies of men could be induced to act from a sense of duty and a love of country, without hope of reward or fear of punishment. When a French general could suffer his division to straggle as they would over the face of the country, with the certainty that they would concentrate upon the

day of battle, he proved that he had soldiers who
were worthy of his trust.

One thing had struck me as curious about these
hussars—that they pronounced French with the
utmost difficulty. I remarked it to the lieutenant
as he rode by my side, and I asked him from what
foreign country his men were recruited, since I
could perceive that they were not Frenchmen.

'My faith, you must not let them hear you say
so,' said he, ' for they would answer you as like as
not by a thrust from their sabres. We are the
premier regiment of the French cavalry, the First
Hussars of Berchény, and, though it is true that
our men are all recruited in Alsace, and few of them
can speak anything but German, they are as good
Frenchmen as Kléber or Kellermann, who came
from the same parts. Our men are all picked, and
our officers,' he added, pulling at his light moustache, ' are the finest in the service.'

The swaggering vanity of the fellow amused me,
for he cocked his busby, swung the blue dolman
which hung from his shoulder, sat his horse, and
clattered his scabbard in a manner which told of
his boyish delight and pride in himself and his

regiment. As I looked at his lithe figure and his
fearless bearing, I could quite imagine that he did
himself no more than justice, while his frank smile
and his merry blue eyes assured me that he would
prove a good comrade. He had himself been
taking observations of me, for he suddenly placed
his hand upon my knee as we rode side by side.

'I trust that the Emperor is not displeased with
you,' said he, with a very grave face.

' I cannot think that he can be so,' I answered,
' for I have come from England to put my services
at his disposal.'

'When the report was presented last night, and
he heard of your presence in that den of thieves,
he was very anxious that you should be brought to
him. Perhaps it is that he wishes you to be guide
to us in England. No doubt you know your way
all over the island.'

The hussar's idea of an island seemed to be
limited to the little patches which lie off the Nor-
man or Breton coast. I tried to explain to him that
this was a great country, not much smaller than
France.

'Well, well,' said he, 'we shall know all about

it presently, for we are going to conquer it. They say in the camp that we shall probably enter London either next Wednesday evening or else on the Thursday morning. We are to have a week for plundering the town, and then one army corps is to take possession of Scotland and another of Ireland.'

His serene confidence made me smile. 'But how do you know you can do all this?' I asked.

'Oh!' said he, 'the Emperor has arranged it.'

'But they have an army, and they are well prepared. They are brave men and they will fight.'

'There would be no use their doing that, for the Emperor is going over himself,' said he; and in the simple answer I understood for the first time the absolute trust and confidence which these soldiers had in their leader. Their feeling for him was fanaticism, and its strength was religion, and never did Mahomet nerve the arms of his believers and strengthen them against pain and death more absolutely than this little grey-coated idol did to those who worshipped him. If he had chosen— and he was more than once upon the point of it— to assert that he was indeed above humanity he

K

would have found millions to grant his claim. You who have heard of him as a stout gentleman in a straw hat, as he was in his later days, may find it hard to understand it, but if you had seen his mangled soldiers still with their dying breath crying out to him, and turning their livid faces towards him as he passed, you would have realised the hold which he had over the minds of men.

'You have been over there?' asked the lieutenant presently, jerking his thumb towards the distant cloud upon the water.

'Yes, I have spent my life there.'

'But why did you stay there when there was such good fighting to be had in the French service?'

' My father was driven out of the country as an aristocrat. It was only after his death that I could offer my sword to the Emperor.'

'You have missed a great deal, but I have no doubt that we shall still have plenty of fine wars. And you think that the English will offer us battle?'

' I have no doubt of it.

'We feared that when they understood that it was the Emperor in person who had come they would throw down their arms. I have heard that there are some fine women over there.'

'The women are beautiful.'

He said nothing, but for some time he squared his shoulders and puffed out his chest, curling up the ends of his little yellow moustache.

'But they will escape in boats,' he muttered at last; and I could see that he had still that picture of a little island in his imagination. 'If they could but see us they might remain. It has been said of the Hussars of Berchény that they can set a whole population running, the women towards us, the men away. We are, as you have no doubt observed, a very fine body of men, and the officers are the pick of the service, though the seniors are hardly up to the same standard as the rest of us.'

With all his self-confidence, this officer did not seem to me to be more than my own age, so I asked him whether he had seen any service. His moustache bristled with indignation at my question, and he looked me up and down with a severe eye.

'I have had the good fortune to be present at nine battles, sir, and at more than forty skirmishes,' said he. 'I have also fought a considerable number of duels, and I can assure you that I am always ready to meet anyone—even a civilian—who may wish to put me to the proof.'

I assured him that he was very fortunate to be so young and yet to have seen so much, upon which his ill-temper vanished as quickly as it came, and he explained that he had served in the Hohenlinden campaign under Moreau, as well as in Napoleon's passage of the Alps, and the campaign of Marengo.

' When you have been with the army for a little time the name of Etienne Gérard will not be so unfamiliar to you,' said he. ' I believe that I may claim to be the hero of one or two little stories which the soldiers love to tell about their camp fires. You will hear of my duel with the six fencing masters, and you will be told how, single-handed, I charged the Austrian Hussars of Graz and brought their silver kettledrum back upon the crupper of my mare. I can assure you that it was not by accident that I was present last night, but it was because Colonel Lasalle was very anxious to be sure of any prisoners whom he might make. As it turned out, however, I only had the one poor chicken-hearted creature, whom I handed over to the provost-marshal.'

'And the other—Toussac ?'

'Ah, he seems to have been a man of another breed. I could have asked nothing better than to have had him at my sword-point. But he has escaped. They caught sight of him and fired a pistol or two, but he knew the bog too well, and they could not follow him.'

'And what will be done to your prisoner ?' I asked.

Lieutenant Gérard shrugged his shoulders.

'I am very sorry for Mademoiselle your cousin,' said he, ' but a fine girl should not love such a man when there are so many gallant soldiers upon the country side. I hear that the Emperor is weary of these endless plottings, and that an example will be made of him.'

Whilst the young hussar and I had been talking we had been cantering down the broad white road, until we were now quite close to the camp, which we could see lying in its arrangement of regiments and brigades beneath us. Our approach lay over the high ground, so that we could see down into

this canvas city, with its interminable lines of
picketed horses, its parks of artillery, and its
swarms of soldiers. In the centre was a clear
space, with one very large tent and a cluster of low
wooden houses in the middle of it, with the tricolour banner waving above them.

'That is the Emperor's quarters, and the
smaller tent there is the headquarters of General
Ney, who commands this corps. You understand
that this is only one of several armies dotted along
from Dunkirk in the north to this, which is the
most southerly. The Emperor goes from one to
the other, inspecting each in its turn, but this is
the main body, and contains most of the picked
troops, so that it is we who see most of him, especially now that the Empress and the Court have
come to Pont de Briques. He is in there at the
present moment,' he added in a hushed voice,
pointing to the great white tent in the centre.

The road into the camp ran through a considerable plain, which was covered by bodies of cavalry
and infantry engaged upon their drill. We had
heard so much in England about Napoleon's troops,
and their feats had appeared so extraordinary, that

"THOSE FELLOWS ON THE BLACK HORSES WITH THE GREAT BLUE RUGS
UPON THEIR CROUPS ARE THE CUIRASSIERS"

my imagination had prepared me for men of very
striking appearance. As a matter of fact, the
ordinary infantry of the line, in their blue coats
and white breeches and gaiters, were quite little
fellows, and even their high brass-covered hats and
red plumes could not make them very imposing.

In spite of their size, however, they were tough
and wiry, and after their eighteen months in camp
they were trained to the highest pitch of perfection.
The ranks were full of veterans, and all the under-
officers had seen much service, while the generals
in command have never been equalled in ability,
so that it was no mean foe which lay with its
menacing eyes fixed upon the distant cliffs of
England. If Pitt had not been able to place the
first navy in the world between the two shores the
history of Europe might be very different to-day.

Lieutenant Gérard, seeing the interest with
which I gazed at the manœuvring troops, was good
enough to satisfy my curiosity about such of them
as approached the road along which we were
journeying.

'Those fellows on the black horses with the great
blue rugs upon their croups are the Cuirassiers,'

said he. 'They are so heavy that they cannot
raise more than a trot, so when they charge we
manage that there shall be a brigade of chasseurs
or hussars behind them to follow up the advantage.'

'Who is the civilian who is inspecting them?'
I asked.

'That is not a civilian, but it is General St.
Cyr, who is one of those whom they called the
Spartans of the Rhine. They were of opinion that
simplicity of life and of dress were part of a good
soldier, and so they would wear no uniform beyond
a simple blue riding coat, such as you see. St.
Cyr is an excellent officer, but he is not popular,
for he seldom speaks to anyone, and he sometimes
shuts himself up for days on end in his tent, where
he plays upon his violin. I think myself that a
soldier is none the worse because he enjoys a glass
of good wine, or has a smart jacket and a few
Brandenburgs across his chest. For my part I do
both, and yet those who know me would tell you
that it has not harmed my soldiering. You see
this infantry upon the left?'

'The men with the yellow facings?'

'Precisely. Those are Oudinot's famous

grenadiers. And the other grenadiers, with the red shoulder-knots and the fur hats strapped above their knapsacks, are the Imperial Guard, the successors of the old Consular Guard who won Marengo for us. Eighteen hundred of them got the cross of honour after the battle. There is the 57th of the line, which has been named "The Terrible," and there is the 7th Light Infantry, who come from the Pyrenees, and who are well known to be the best marchers and the greatest rascals in the army. The light cavalry in green are the Horse Chasseurs of the Guard, sometimes called the Guides, who are said to be the Emperor's favourite troops, although he makes a great mistake if he prefers them to the Hussars of Berchény. The other cavalry with the green pelisses are also chasseurs, but I cannot tell from here what regiment they are. Their colonel handles them admirably. They are moving to a flank in open column of half-squadrons and then wheeling into line to charge. We could not do it better ourselves. And now, Monsieur de Laval, here we are at the gates of the Camp of Boulogne, and it is my duty to take you straight to the Emperor's quarters.'

CHAPTER X

THE ANTE-ROOM

THE camp of Boulogne contained at that time one hundred and fifty thousand infantry, with fifty thousand cavalry, so that its population was second only to Paris among the cities of France. It was divided into four sections, the right camp, the left camp, the camp of Wimereux, and the camp of Ambleteuse, the whole being about a mile in depth, and extending along the seashore for a length of about seven miles. On the land side it was open, but on the sea side it was fringed by powerful batteries containing mortars and cannon of a size never seen before. These batteries were placed along the edges of the high cliffs, and their lofty position increased their range, and enabled them to drop their missiles upon the decks of the English ships.

It was a pretty sight to ride through the camp,

for the men had been there for more than a year, and had done all that was possible to decorate and ornament their tents. Most of them had little gardens in front or around them, and the sun-burned fellows might be seen as we passed kneeling in their shirt-sleeves with their spuds and their watering-cans in the midst of their flower-beds. Others sat in the sunshine at the openings of the tents tying up their queues, pipe-claying their belts, and polishing their arms, hardly bestowing a glance upon us as we passed, for patrols of cavalry were coming and going in every direction. The endless lines were formed into streets, with their names printed up upon boards. Thus we had passed through the Rue d'Arcola, the Rue de Kléber, the Rue d'Égypte, and the Rue d'Artillerie Volante, before we found ourselves in the great central square in which the headquarters of the army were situated.

The Emperor at this time used to sleep at a village called Pont de Briques, some four miles inland, but his days were spent at the camp, and his continual councils of war were held there. Here also were his ministers, and the generals of the army corps which were scattered up and down the coast came thither to make their reports and to receive their orders. For these consultations a plain wooden house had been constructed containing one very large room and three small ones. The pavilion which we had observed from the Downs served as an ante-chamber to the house, in which those who sought audience with the Emperor might assemble. It was at the door of this, where a strong guard of grenadiers announced Napoleon's presence, that my guardian sprang down from his horse and signed to me to follow his example. An officer of the guard took our names and returned to us accompanied by General Duroc, a thin, hard, dry man of forty, with a formal manner and a suspicious eye.

'Is this Monsieur Louis de Laval?' he asked, with a stiff smile.

I bowed.

'The Emperor is very anxious to see you. You are no longer needed, Lieutenant.'

'I am personally responsible for bringing him safely, General.'

'Very good. You may come in, if you prefer

it!' And he passed us into the huge tent, which was unfurnished, save for a row of wooden benches round the sides. A number of men in naval and military uniforms were seated upon these, and numerous groups were standing about chatting in subdued tones. At the far end was a door which led into the Imperial council chamber. Now and then I saw some man in official dress walk up to this door, scratch gently upon it with his nail, and then, as it instantly opened, slip discreetly through, closing it softly behind him. Over the whole assembly there hung an air of the Court rather than of the camp, an atmosphere of awe and of reverence which was the more impressive when it affected these bluff soldiers and sailors. The Emperor had seemed to me to be formidable in the distance, but I found him even more overwhelming now that he was close at hand.

'You need have no fears, Monsieur de Laval,' said my companion. 'You are going to have a good reception.'

'How do you know that?'

'From General Duroc's manner. In these

cursed Courts, if the Emperor smiles upon you everyone smiles, down to that flunkey in the red velvet coat yonder. But if the Emperor frowns, why, you have only to look at the face of the man who washes the Imperial plates, and you will see the frown reflected upon it. And the worst of it is that, if you are a plain-witted man, you may never find out what earned you either the frown or the smile. That is why I had rather wear the shoulder-straps of a lieutenant, and be at the side of my squadron, with a good horse between my knees and my sabre clanking against my stirrup-iron, than have Monsieur Talleyrand's grand hotel in the Rue Saint Florentin, and his hundred thousand livres of income.'

I was still wondering whether the hussar could be right, and if the smile with which Duroc had greeted me could mean that the Emperor's intentions towards me were friendly, when a very tall and handsome young man, in a brilliant uniform, came towards me. In spite of the change in his dress, I recognised him at once as the General Savary who had commanded the expedition of the night before.

'Well, Monsieur de Laval,' said he, shaking hands with me very pleasantly, 'you have heard, no doubt, that this fellow Toussac has escaped us. He was really the only one whom we were anxious to seize, for the other is evidently a mere dupe and dreamer. But we shall have him yet, and between ourselves we shall keep a very strict guard upon the Emperor's person until we do, for Master Toussac is not a man to be despised.'

I seemed to feel his great rough thumb upon my chin as I answered that I thought he was a very dangerous man indeed.

'The Emperor will see you presently,' said Savary. 'He is very busy this morning, but he bade me say that you should have an audience.' He smiled and passed on.

'Assuredly you are getting on,' whispered Gérard. 'There are a good many men here who would risk something to have Savary address them as he addressed you. The Emperor is certainly going to do something for you. But attention, friend, for here is Monsieur de Talleyrand himself coming towards us.'

A singular-looking person was shuffling in our

direction. He was a man about fifty years of age, largely made about the shoulders and chest, but stooping a good deal, and limping heavily in one leg. He walked slowly, leaning upon a silver-headed stick, and his sober suit of black, with silk stockings of the same hue, looked strangely staid among the brilliant uniforms which surrounded him. But in spite of his plain dress there was an expression of great authority upon his shrewd face, and every one drew back with bows and salutes as he moved across the tent.

'Monsieur Louis de Laval?' said he, as he stopped in front of me, and his cold grey eyes played over me from head to heel.

I bowed, and with some coldness, for I shared the dislike which my father used to profess for this unfrocked priest and perjured politician; but his manner was so polished and engaging that it was hard to hold out against it.

'I knew your cousin de Rohan very well indeed,' said he. 'We were two rascals together when the world was not quite so serious as it is at present. I believe that you are related to the Cardinal de Montmorency de Laval, who is also an old friend

of mine.   I understand that you are about to offer
your services to the Emperor ? '

'I have come from England for that purpose, sir.'

'And met with some little adventure immediately upon your arrival, as I understand.   I have
heard the story of the worthy police agent, the
two Jacobins, and the lonely hut.   Well, you have
seen the danger to which the Emperor is exposed,
and it may make you the more zealous in his
service.   Where is your uncle, Monsieur Bernac ? '

'He is at the Castle of Grosbois.'

'Do you know him well ? '

'I had not seen him until yesterday.'

'He is a very useful servant of the Emperor, but
—but—' he inclined his head downward to my ear,
'some more congenial service will be found for you,
Monsieur de Laval,' and so, with a bow, he whisked
round, and tapped his way across the tent again.

'Why, my friend, you are certainly destined
for something great,' said the hussar lieutenant.
'Monsieur de Talleyrand does not waste his smiles
and his bows, I promise you.   He knows which
way the wind blows before he flies his kite, and I
foresee that I shall be asking for your interest

L

to get me my captaincy in this English campaign.
Ah, the council of war is at an end.'

As he spoke the inner door at the end of the
great tent opened, and a small knot of men came
through dressed in the dark blue coats, with trimmings of gold oak-leaves, which marked the marshals of the Empire. They were, all but one, men
who had hardly reached their middle age, and who,
in any other army, might have been considered
fortunate if they had gained the command of a
regiment; but the continuous wars and the open
system by which rules of seniority yielded to merit
had opened up a rapid career to a successful soldier.
Each carried his curved cocked hat under his arm,
and now, leaning upon their sword-hilts, they fell
into a little circle and chatted eagerly among themselves.

'You are a man of family, are you not?' asked
my hussar.

'I am of the same blood as the de Rohans and
the Montmorencies.'

'So I had understood. Well, then, you will
understand that there have been some changes in
this country when I tell you that those men, who,

under the Emperor, are the greatest in the country
have been the one a waiter, the next a wine smuggler, the next a cooper of barrels, and the next a
house painter. Those are the trades which gave
us Murat, Masséna, Ney, and Lannes.'

Aristocrat as I was, no names had ever thrilled
me as those did, and I eagerly asked him to point
me out each of these famous soldiers.

'Oh, there are many famous soldiers in the
room,' said he. 'Besides,' he added, twisting his
moustache, 'there may be junior officers here who
have it in them to rise higher than any of them.
But there is Ney to the right.'

I saw a man with close-cropped red hair and a
large square-jowled face, such as I have seen upon
an English prize-fighter.

'We call him Peter the Red, and sometimes the
Red Lion, in the army,' said my companion. 'He
is said to be the bravest man in the army, though
I cannot admit that he is braver than some other
people whom I could mention. Still he is un-
doubtedly a very good leader.'

'And the general next him?' I asked. 'Why
does he carry his head all upon one side?'

'That is General Lannes, and he carries his head upon his left shoulder because he was shot through the neck at the siege of St. Jean d'Acre. He is a Gascon, like myself, and I fear that he gives some ground to those who accuse my countrymen of being a little talkative and quarrelsome. But monsieur smiles?'

'You are mistaken.'

'I thought that perhaps something which I had said might have amused monsieur. I thought that possibly he meant that Gascons really were quarrelsome, instead of being, as I contend, the mildest race in France—an opinion which I am always ready to uphold in any way which may be suggested. But, as I say, Lannes is a very valiant man, though, occasionally, perhaps, a trifle hot-headed. The next man is Auguereau.'

I looked with interest upon the hero of Castiglione, who had taken command upon the one occasion when Napoleon's heart and spirit had failed him. He was a man, I should judge, who would shine rather in war than in peace, for, with his long goat's face and his brandy nose, he looked, in spite of his golden oak-leaves, just such a long-legged, vulgar, swaggering, foul-mouthed old soldier as every barrack-room can show. He was an older man than the others, and his sudden promotion had come too late for him to change. He was always the Corporal of the Prussian Guard under the hat of the French Marshal.

'Yes, yes; he is a rough fellow,' said Gérard, in answer to my remark. 'He is one of those whom the Emperor had to warn that he wished them to be soldiers only with the army. He and Rapp and Lefebvre, with their big boots and their clanking sabres, were too much for the Empress's drawing-room at the Tuileries. There is Vandamme also, the dark man with the heavy face. Heaven help the English village that he finds his quarters in! It was he who got into trouble because he broke the jaw of a Westphalian priest who could not find him a second bottle of Tokay.'

'And that is Murat, I suppose?'

'Yes; that is Murat with the black whiskers and the red, thick lips, and the brown of Egypt upon his face. He is the man for me! My word, when you have seen him raving in front of a brigade of light cavalry, with his plumes tossing and

his sabre flashing, you would not wish to see anything finer. I have known a square of grenadiers
break and scatter at the very sight of him. In
Egypt the Emperor kept away from him, for the
Arabs would not look at the little General when this
fine horseman and swordsman was before them.
In my opinion Lasalle is the better light cavalry
officer, but there is no one whom the men will
follow as they do Murat.'

'And who is the stern-looking man, leaning on
the Oriental sword ? '

'Oh, that is Soult! He is the most obstinate
man in the world. He argues with the Emperor.
The handsome man beside him is Junot, and Bernadotte is leaning against the tent-pole.'

I looked with interest at the extraordinary face
of this adventurer, who, after starting with a musket
and a knapsack in the ranks, was not contented
with the bâton of a marshal, but passed on afterwards to grasp the sceptre of a king. And it might
be said of him that, unlike his fellows, he gained
his throne in spite of Napoleon rather than by his
aid. Any man who looked at his singular pronounced features, the swarthiness of which pro-

claimed his half Spanish origin, must have read in his flashing black eyes and in that huge aggressive nose that he was reserved for a strange destiny. Of all the fierce and masterful men who surrounded the Emperor there was none with greater gifts, and none, also, whose ambitions he more distrusted, than those of Jules Bernadotte.

And yet, fierce and masterful as these men were, having, as Augereau boasted, fear neither of God nor of the devil, there was something which thrilled or cowed them in the pale smile or black frown of the little man who ruled them. For, as I watched them, there suddenly came over the assembly a start and hush such as you see in a boys' school when the master enters unexpectedly, and there near the open doors of his headquarters stood the master himself. Even without that sudden silence, and the scramble to their feet of those upon the benches, I felt that I should have known instantly that he was present. There was a pale luminosity about his ivory face which drew the eye towards it, and though his dress might be the plainest of a hundred, his appearance would be the first which one would notice. There he was,

with his little plump, heavy-shouldered figure, his
green coat with the red collar and cuffs, his white,
well-formed legs, his sword with the gilt hilt and
the tortoise-shell scabbard. His head was uncovered,
showing his thin hair of a ruddy chestnut colour.
Under one arm was the flat cocked hat with the
twopenny tricolour rosette, which was already
reproduced in his pictures. In his right hand he
held a little riding switch with a metal head. He
walked slowly forward, his face immutable, his eyes
fixed steadily before him, measured, inexorable, the
very personification of Destiny.

'Admiral Bruix!'

I do not know if that voice thrilled through
every one as it did through me. Never had I heard
anything more harsh, more menacing, more
sinister. From under his puckered brows his light-
blue eyes glanced swiftly round with a sweep like
a sabre.

'I am here, Sire!' A dark, grizzled, middle-
aged man, in a naval uniform, had advanced from
the throng. Napoleon took three quick little steps
towards him in so menacing a fashion, that I saw
the weather-stained cheeks of the sailor turn a

shade paler, and he gave a helpless glance round him, as if for assistance.

'How comes it, Admiral Bruix,' cried the Emperor, in the same terrible rasping voice, 'that you did not obey my commands last night?'

'I could see that a westerly gale was coming up, Sire. I knew that——,' he could hardly speak for his agitation, 'I knew that if the ships went out with this lee shore——'

'What right have you to judge, sir?' cried the Emperor, in a cold fury of indignation. 'Do you conceive that your judgment is to be placed against mine?'

'In matters of navigation, Sire.'

'In no matters whatsoever.'

'But the tempest, Sire! Did it not prove me to be in the right?'

'What! You still dare to bandy words with me?'

'When I have justice on my side.'

There was a hush amidst all the great audience; such a heavy silence as comes only when many are waiting, and all with bated breath. The Emperor's face was terrible. His cheeks were of a greenish, livid tint, and there was a singular rotary movement of the muscles of his forehead. It was the countenance of an epileptic. He raised the whip to his shoulder, and took a step towards the admiral.

'You insolent rascal!' he hissed. It was the Italian word *coglione* which he used, and I observed that as his feelings overcame him his French became more and more that of a foreigner.

For a moment he seemed to be about to slash the sailor across the face with his whip. The latter took a step back, and clapped his hand to his sword.

'Have a care, Sire,' said he.

For a few instants the tension was terrible. Then Napoleon brought the whip down with a sharp crack against his own thigh.

'Vice-Admiral Magon,' he cried, 'you will in future receive all orders connected with the fleet. Admiral Bruix, you will leave Boulogne in twenty-four hours and withdraw to Holland. Where is Lieutenant Gérard, of the Hussars of Berchény?'

My companion's gauntlet sprang to his busby.

'I ordered you to bring Monsieur Louis de Laval from the castle of Grosbois.'

'He is here, Sire.'

'Good! You may retire.'

The lieutenant saluted, whisked round upon his heel, and clattered away, whilst the Emperor's blue eyes were turned upon me. I had often heard the phrase of eyes looking through you, but that piercing gaze did really give one the feeling that it penetrated to one's inmost thoughts. But the sternness had all melted out of it, and I read a great gentleness and kindness in their expression.

'You have come to serve me, Monsieur de Laval?'

'Yes, Sire.'

'You have been some time in making up your mind.'

'I was not my own master, Sire.'

'Your father was an aristocrat?'

'Yes, Sire.'

'And a supporter of the Bourbons?'

'Yes, Sire.'

'You will find that in France now there are no aristocrats and no Jacobins; but that we are all

Frenchmen working for the glory of our country.
Have you seen Louis de Bourbon?'

'I have seen him once, Sire?'

'An insignificant-looking man, is he not?'

'No, Sire, I thought him a fine-looking man.'

For a moment I saw a hard gleam of resentment in those changing blue eyes. Then he put
out his hand and pinched one of my ears.

'Monsieur de Laval was not born to be a
courtier,' said he. 'Well, well, Louis de Bourbon
will find that he cannot gain a throne by writing
proclamations in London and signing them Louis.
For my part, I found the crown of France lying
upon the ground, and I lifted it upon my sword-
point.'

'You have lifted France with your sword also,
Sire,' said Talleyrand, who stood at his elbow.

Napoleon looked at his famous minister, and I
seemed to read suspicion in his eyes. Then he
turned to his secretary.

'I leave Monsieur de Laval in your hands, de
Meneval,' said he. 'I desire to see him in the
council chamber after the inspection of the artillery.'

THEN HE PUT OUT HIS HAND AND PINCHED ONE OF MY EARS

CHAPTER XI

THE SECRETARY

EMPEROR, generals, and officials all streamed away
to the review, leaving me with a gentle-looking,
large-eyed man in a black suit with very white
cambric ruffles, who introduced himself to me as
Monsieur de Meneval, private secretary to His
Majesty.

'We must get some food, Monsieur de Laval,'
said he. 'It is always well, if you have anything
to do with the Emperor, to get your food whenever
you have the chance. It may be many hours
before he takes a meal, and if you are in his
presence you have to fast also. I assure you that
I have nearly fainted from hunger and from thirst.'

'But how does the Emperor manage himself?'
I asked. This Monsieur de Meneval had such a
kindly human appearance that I already felt much
at my ease with him.

'Oh, he, he is a man of iron, Monsieur de Laval. We must not set our watches by his. I have known him work for eighteen hours on end and take nothing but a cup or two of coffee. He wears everybody out around him. Even the soldiers cannot keep up with him. I assure you that I look upon it as the very highest honour to have charge of his papers, but there are times when it is very trying all the same. Sometimes it is eleven o'clock at night, Monsieur de Laval, and I am writing to his dictation with my head aching for want of sleep. It is dreadful work, for he dictates as quickly as he can talk, and he never repeats anything. "Now, Meneval," says he suddenly, "we shall stop here and have a good night's rest." And then, just as I am congratulating myself, he adds, "and we shall continue with the dictation at three to-morrow morning." That is what he means by a good night's rest.'

'But has he no hours for his meals, Monsieur de Meneval?' I asked, as I accompanied the unhappy secretary out of the tent.

'Oh, yes, he has hours, but he will not observe them. You see that it is already long after dinner time, but he has gone to this review. After the review something else will probably take up his attention, and then something else, until suddenly in the evening it will occur to him that he has had no dinner. " My dinner, Constant, this instant ! " he will cry, and poor Constant has to see that it is there.'

' But it must be unfit to eat by that time,' said I.

The secretary laughed in the discreet way of a man who has always been obliged to control his emotions.

' This is the Imperial kitchen,' said he, indicating a large tent just outside the headquarters. ' Here is Borel, the second cook, at the door. How many pullets to-day, Borel ? '

' Ah, Monsieur de Meneval, it is heartrending,' cried the cook. ' Behold them ! ' and, drawing back the flap of the entrance, he showed us seven dishes, each of them containing a cold fowl. ' The eighth is now on the fire and done to a turn, but I hear that His Majesty has started for the review, so we must put on a ninth.'

' That is how it is managed,' said my companion, as we turned from the tent. ' I have known

twenty-three fowls got ready for him before he
asked for his meal. That day he called for his
dinner at eleven at night. He cares little what he
eats or drinks, but he will not be kept waiting.
Half a bottle of Chambertin, a red mullet, or a
pullet à la Marengo satisfy every need, but it is
unwise to put pastry or cream upon the table,
because he is as likely as not to eat it before the
fowl. Ah, that is a curious sight, is it not?'

I had halted with an exclamation of astonishment. A groom was cantering a very beautiful
Arab horse down one of the lanes between the
tents. As it passed, a grenadier who was standing
with a small pig under his arm hurled it down
under the feet of the horse. The pig squealed
vigorously and scuttled away, but the horse
cantered on without changing its step.

'What does that mean?' I asked.

'That is Jardin, the head groom, breaking in a
charger for the Emperor's use. They are first
trained by having a cannon fired in their ears, then
they are struck suddenly by heavy objects, and
finally they have the test of the pig being thrown
under their feet. The Emperor has not a very

firm seat, and he very often loses himself in
a reverie when he is riding, so it might not be
very safe if the horse were not well trained. Do
you see that young man asleep at the door of a
tent ? '

' Yes, I see him.'

' You would not think that he is at the present
moment serving the Emperor ? '

' It seems a very easy service.'

' I wish all our services were as easy, Monsieur
de Laval. That is Joseph Linden, whose foot is
the exact size of the Emperor's. He wears his new
boots and shoes for three days before they are
given to his master. You can see by the gold
buckles that he has a pair on at the present
moment. Ah, Monsieur de Caulaincourt, will you
not join us at dinner in my tent ? '

A tall, handsome man, very elegantly dressed,
came across and greeted us. ' It is rare to find
you at rest, Monsieur de Meneval. I have no very
light task myself as head of the household, but I
think I have more leisure than you. Have we
time for dinner before the Emperor returns ? '

' Yes, yes; here is the tent, and everything

M

ready. We can see when the Emperor returns,
and be in the room before he can reach it. This
is camp fare, Monsieur de Laval, but no doubt you
will excuse it.'

For my own part I had an excellent appetite
for the cutlets and the salad, but what I relished
above all was to hear the talk of my companions,
for I was full of curiosity as to everything which
concerned this singular man, whose genius had
elevated him so rapidly to the highest position in
the world. The head of his household discussed
him with an extraordinary frankness.

'What do they say of him in England, Monsieur
de Laval?' he asked.

'Nothing very good.'

'So I have gathered from their papers. They
drive the Emperor frantic, and yet he will insist
upon reading them. I am willing to lay a wager
that the very first thing which he does when he
enters London will be to send cavalry detachments
to the various newspaper offices, and to endeavour
to seize the editors.'

'And the next?'

'The next,' said he, laughing, 'will be to issue

a long proclamation to prove that we have
conquered England entirely for the good of the
English, and very much against our own inclina-
tions. And then, perhaps, the Emperor will allow
the English to understand that, if they absolutely
demand a Protestant for a ruler, it is possible that
there are a few little points in which he differs
from Holy Church.'

'Too bad! Too bad!' cried de Meneval,
looking amused and yet rather frightened at his
companion's audacity. 'No doubt for state reasons
the Emperor had to tamper a little with Mahom-
medanism, and I daresay he would attend this
Church of St. Paul's as readily as he did the
Mosque at Cairo; but it would not do for a ruler
to be a bigot. After all, the Emperor has to think
for all.'

'He thinks too much,' said Caulaincourt,
gravely. 'He thinks so much that other people
in France are getting out of the way of thinking at
all. You know what I mean, de Meneval, for you
have seen it as much as I have.'

'Yes, yes,' answered the secretary. 'He
certainly does not encourage originality among

those who surround him. I have heard him say
many a time that he desired nothing but mediocrity, which was a poor compliment, it must be
confessed, to us who have the honour of serving
him.'

'A clever man at his Court shows his cleverness
best by pretending to be dull,' said Caulaincourt,
with some bitterness.

'And yet there are many famous characters
there,' I remarked.

'If so, it is only by concealing their characters
that they remain there. His ministers are clerks,
his generals are superior aides-de-camp. They
are all agents. You have this wonderful man in
the middle, and all around you have so many
mirrors which reflect different sides of him. In
one you see him as a financier, and you call it
Lebrun. In another you have him as a gen-
darme, and you name it Savary or Fouché. In
yet another he figures as a diplomatist, and is
called Talleyrand. You see different figures, but it
is really the same man. There is a Monsieur de
Caulaincourt, for example, who arranges the
household ; but he cannot dismiss a servant with-

out permission. It is still always the Emperor.
And he plays upon us. We must confess, de
Meneval, that he plays upon us. In nothing else
do I see so clearly his wonderful cleverness. He
will not let us be too friendly lest we combine.
He has set his Marshals against each other until
there are hardly two of them on speaking terms.
Look how Davoust hates Bernadotte, or Lannes
and Bessières, or Ney and Masséna. It is all they
can do to keep their sabres in their sheaths when
they meet. And then he knows our weak points.
Savary's thirst for money, Cambacérès's vanity,
Duroc's bluntness, Berthier's foolishness, Maret's
insipidity, Talleyrand's mania for speculation, they
are all so many tools in his hand. I do not
know what my own greatest weakness may be,
but I am sure that he does, and that he uses his
knowledge.'

'But how he must work ! ' I exclaimed.

' Ah, you may say so,' said de Meneval. ' What
energy ! Eighteen hours out of twenty-four for
weeks on end. He has presided over the Legislative
Council until they were fainting at their desks. As
to me, he will be the death of me, just as he wore

out de Bourrienne; but I will die at my post
without a murmur, for if he is hard upon us he is
hard upon himself also.'

'He was the man for France,' said de Caulaincourt. 'He is the very genius of system and of
order, and of discipline. When one remembers the
chaos in which our poor country found itself after
the Revolution, when no one would be governed
and everyone wanted to govern someone else, you
will understand that only Napoleon could have
saved us. We were all longing for something fixed
to secure ourselves to, and then we came upon this
iron pillar of a man. And what a man he was in
those days, Monsieur de Laval! You see him now
when he has got all that he can want. He is good-
humoured and easy. But at that time he had got
nothing, but coveted everything. His glance frightened women. He walked the streets like a wolf.
People looked after him as he passed. His face was
quite different—it was craggy, hollow-cheeked, with
an oblique menacing gaze, and the jaws of a pike.
Oh, yes, this little Lieutenant Buonaparte from the
Military School of Brienne was a singular figure.
"There is a man," said I, when I saw him, "who

will sit upon a throne or kneel upon a scaffold." And
now look at him ! '

'And that is ten years ago,' I exclaimed.

'Only ten years, and they have brought him
from a barrack-room to the Tuileries. But he was
born for it. You could not keep him down. De
Bourrienne told me that when he was a little fellow
at Brienne he had the grand Imperial manner, and
would praise or blame, glare or smile, exactly as he
does now. Have you seen his mother, Monsieur de
Laval ? She is a tragedy queen, tall, stern, reserved, silent. There is the spring from which
he flowed.'

I could see in the gentle, spaniel-eyes of the
secretary that he was disturbed by the frankness of
de Caulaincourt's remarks.

'You can tell that we do not live under a very
terrible tyranny, Monsieur de Laval,' said he, 'or
we should hardly venture to discuss our ruler so
frankly. The fact is that we have said nothing
which he would not have listened to with pleasure
and perhaps with approval. He has his little frail-
ties, or he would not be human, but take his quali-
ties as a ruler and I would ask you if there has

ever been a man who has justified the choice of a
nation so completely. He works harder than any
of his subjects. He is a general beloved by his soldiers. He is a master beloved by his servants. He
never has a holiday, and he is always ready for his
work. There is not under the roof of the Tuileries
a more abstemious eater or drinker. He educated
his brothers at his own expense when he was a very
poor man, and he has caused even his most distant
relatives to share in his prosperity. In a word, he
is economical, hard-working, and temperate. We
read in the London papers about this Prince of
Wales, Monsieur de Laval, and I do not think
that he comes very well out of the comparison.'

I thought of the long record of Brighton scandals, London scandals, Newmarket scandals, and I
had to leave George undefended.

'As I understand it,' said I, 'it is not the
Emperor's private life, but his public ambition, that
the English attack.'

'The fact is,' said de Caulaincourt, 'that the
Emperor knows, and we all know, that there is not
room enough in the world for both France and
England. One or other must be supreme. If

England were once crushed we could then lay the foundations of a permanent peace. Italy is ours. Austria we can crush again as we have crushed her before. Germany is divided. Russia can expand to the south and east. America we can take at our leisure, finding our pretext in Louisiana or in Canada. There is a world empire waiting for us, and there is the only thing that stops us.' He pointed out through the opening of the tent at the broad blue Channel.

Far away, like snow-white gulls in the distance, were the sails of the blockading fleet. I thought again of what I had seen the night before—the lights of the ships upon the sea and the glow of the camp upon the shore. The powers of the land and of the ocean were face to face whilst a waiting world stood round to see what would come of it.

CHAPTER XII

THE MAN OF ACTION

DE MENEVAL's tent had been pitched in such a
way that he could overlook the Royal headquarters,
but whether it was that we were too absorbed in
the interest of our conversation, or that the
Emperor had used the other entrance in returning
from the review, we were suddenly startled by the
appearance of a captain dressed in the green jacket
of the Chasseurs of the Guard, who had come to
say that Napoleon was waiting for his secretary.
Poor de Meneval's face turned as white as his
beautiful ruffles as he sprang to his feet, hardly
able to speak for agitation.

'I should have been there!' he gasped. 'Oh,
what a misfortune! Monsieur de Caulaincourt,
you must excuse me! Where is my hat and my
sword? Come, Monsieur de Laval, not an instant
is to be lost!'

I could judge from the terror of de Meneval, as well as from the scene which I had witnessed with Admiral Bruix, what the influence was which the Emperor exercised over those who were around him. They were never at their ease, always upon the brink of a catastrophe, encouraged one day only to be rudely rebuffed the next, bullied in public and slighted in private, and yet, in spite of it all, the singular fact remains that they loved him and served him as no monarch has been loved and served.

'Perhaps I had best stay here,' said I, when we had come to the ante-chamber, which was still crowded with people.

'No, no, I am responsible for you. You must come with me. Oh, I trust he is not offended with me! How could he have got in without my seeing him?'

My frightened companion scratched at the door, which was opened instantly by Roustem the Mameluke, who guarded it within. The room into which we passed was of considerable size, but was furnished with extreme simplicity. It was papered of a silver-grey colour, with a sky-blue ceiling, in

the centre of which was the Imperial eagle in gold,
holding a thunderbolt. In spite of the warm
weather, a large fire was burning at one side, and
the air was heavy with heat and the aromatic
smell of aloes. In the middle of the room was a
large oval table covered with green cloth and
littered with a number of letters and papers. A
raised writing-desk was at one side of the table,
and behind it in a green morocco chair with curved
arms there sat the Emperor. A number of officials
were standing round the walls, but he took no
notice of them. In his hand he had a small pen-
knife, with which he whittled the wooden knob at
the end of his chair. He glanced up as we entered,
and shook his head coldly at de Meneval.

'I have had to wait for you, Monsieur de
Meneval,' said he. 'I cannot remember that I
ever waited for my late secretary de Bourrienne.
That is enough! No excuses! Take this report
which I have written in your absence, and make a
copy of it.'

Poor de Meneval took the paper with a shaking
hand, and carried it to the little side table which
was reserved for his use. Napoleon rose and

paced slowly up and down the room with his hands behind his back, and his big round head stooping a little forwards. It was certainly as well that he had a secretary, for I observed that in writing this single document he had spattered the whole place with ink, and it was obvious that he had twice used his white kerseymere knee-breeches as a pen-wiper. As for me, I stood quietly beside Roustem at the door, and he took not the slightest notice of my presence.

'Well,' he cried presently, 'is it ready, de Meneval? We have something more to do.'

The secretary half turned in his chair, and his face was more agitated than ever.

'If it please you, Sire——' he stammered.

'Well, well, what is the matter now?'

'If it please you, Sire, I find some little difficulty in reading what you have written.'

'Tut, tut, sir. You see what the report is about.'

'Yes, Sire, it is about forage for the cavalry horses.'

Napoleon smiled, and the action made his face look quite boyish.

'You remind me of Cambacérès, de Meneval. When I wrote him an account of the battle of Marengo, he thought that my letter was a rough plan of the engagement. It is incredible how much difficulty you appear to have in reading what I write. This document has nothing to do with cavalry horses, but it contains the instructions to Admiral Villeneuve as to the concentration of his fleet so as to obtain command of the Channel. Give it to me and I will read it to you.'

He snatched the paper up in the quick impulsive way which was characteristic of him. But after a long fierce stare he crumpled it up and hurled it under the table.

'I will dictate it to you,' said he; and, pacing up and down the long room, he poured forth a torrent of words, which poor de Meneval, his face shining with his exertions, strove hard to put upon paper. As he grew excited by his own ideas, Napoleon's voice became shriller, his step faster, and he seized his right cuff in the fingers of the same hand, and twisted his right arm in the singular epileptic gesture which was peculiar to him. But

his thoughts and plans were so admirably clear
that even I, who knew nothing of the matter, could
readily follow them, while above all I was impressed
by the marvellous grasp of fact which enabled him
to speak with confidence, not only of the line-of-
battle ships, but of the frigates, sloops, and brigs
at Ferrol, Rochefort, Cadiz, Carthagena, and Brest,
with the exact strength of each in men and in
guns; while the names and force of the English
vessels were equally at his fingers' ends. Such
familiarity would have been remarkable in a naval
officer, but when I thought that this question of
the ships was only one out of fifty with which this
man had to deal, I began to realise the immense
grasp of that capacious mind. He did not appear
to be paying the least attention to me, but it
seems that he was really watching me closely, for
he turned upon me when he had finished his
dictation.

'You appear to be surprised, Monsieur de Laval,
that I should be able to transact my naval business
without having my minister of marine at my elbow;
but it is one of my rules to know and to do things
for myself. Perhaps if these good Bourbons had

had the same habit they would not now be living amidst the fogs of England.'

'One must have your Majesty's memory in order to do it,' I observed.

'It is the result of system,' said he. 'It is as if I had drawers in my brain, so that when I opened one I could close the others. It is seldom that I fail to find what I want there. I have a poor memory for names or dates, but an excellent one for facts or faces. There is a good deal to bear in mind, Monsieur de Laval. For example, I have, as you have seen, my one little drawer full of the ships upon the sea. I have another which contains all the harbours and forts of France. As an example, I may tell you that when my minister of war was reading me a report of all the coast defences, I was able to point out to him that he had omitted two guns in a battery near Ostend. In yet another of my brain-drawers I have the regiments of France. Is that drawer in order, Marshal Berthier?'

A clean-shaven man, who had stood biting his nails in the window, bowed at the Emperor's question.

'I am sometimes tempted to believe, Sire, that you know the name of every man in the ranks,' said he.

'I think that I know most of my old Egyptian grumblers,' said he. 'And then, Monsieur de Laval, there is another drawer for canals, bridges, roads, manufactures, and every detail of internal administration. The law, finance, Italy, the Colonies, Holland, all these things demand drawers of their own. In these days, Monsieur de Laval, France asks something more of its ruler than that he should carry eight yards of ermine with dignity, or ride after a stag in the forest of Fontainebleau.'

I thought of the helpless, gentle, pompous Louis whom my father had once taken me to visit, and I understood that France, after her convulsions and her sufferings, did indeed require another and a stronger head.

'Do you not think so, Monsieur de Laval?' asked the Emperor. He had halted for a moment by the fire, and was grinding his dainty gold-buckled shoe into one of the burning logs.

'You have come to a very wise decision,' said he when I had answered his question. 'But you have

N

always been of this way of thinking, have you not? Is it not true that you once defended me when some young Englishman was drinking toasts to my downfall at an inn in this village in which you lived?'

I remembered the incident, although I could not imagine how it had reached his ears.

'Why should you have done this?'

'I did it on impulse, Sire.'

'On impulse!' he cried, in a tone of contempt. 'I do not know what people mean when they say that they do things upon impulse. In Charenton things are doubtless done upon impulse, but not amongst sane people. Why should you risk your life over there in defending me when at the time you had nothing to hope for from me?'

'It was because I felt that you stood for France, Sire.'

During this conversation he had still walked up and down the room, twisting his right arm about, and occasionally looking at one or other of us with his eyeglass, for his sight was so weak that he always needed a single glass indoors and binoculars outside. Sometimes he stopped and helped himself to great pinches of snuff from a

tortoise-shell box, but I observed that none of it
ever reached his nose, for he dropped it all from
between his fingers on to his waistcoat and the
floor. My answer seemed to please him, for he
suddenly seized my ear and pulled it with considerable violence.

'You are quite right, my friend,' said he. 'I
stand for France just as Frederic the Second stood
for Prussia. I will make her the great Power of
the world, so that every monarch in Europe will
find it necessary to keep a palace in Paris, and they
will all come to hold the train at the coronation of
my descendants—' a spasm of pain passed suddenly
over his face. 'My God! for whom am I building? Who will be my descendants?' I heard
him mutter, and he passed his hand over his
forehead.

'Do they seem frightened in England about
my approaching invasion?' he asked suddenly.
'Have you heard them express fears lest I get
across the Channel?'

I was forced in truth to say that the only fears
which I had ever heard expressed were lest he
should not get across.

'The soldiers are very jealous that the sailors should always have the honour,' said I.

'But they have a very small army.'

'Nearly every man is a volunteer, Sire.'

'Pooh, conscripts!' he cried, and made a motion with his hands as if to sweep them from before him. 'I will land with a hundred thousand men in Kent or in Sussex. I will fight a great battle which I will win with a loss of ten thousand men. On the third day I shall be in London. I will seize the statesmen, the bankers, the merchants, the newspaper men. I will impose an indemnity of a hundred millions of their pounds. I will favour the poor at the expense of the rich, and so I shall have a party. I will detach Scotland and Ireland by giving them constitutions which will put them in a superior condition to England. Thus I will sow dissensions everywhere. Then as a price for leaving the island I will claim their fleet and their colonies. In this way I shall secure the command of the world to France for at least a century to come.'

In this short sketch I could perceive the quality which I have since heard remarked in Napoleon, that his mind could both conceive a large scheme, and at the same time evolve those practical details which would seem to bring it within the bounds of possibility. One instant it would be a wild dream of overrunning the East. The next it was a schedule of the ships, the ports, the stores, the troops, which would be needed to turn dream into fact. He gripped the heart of a question with the same decision which made him strike straight for an enemy's capital. The soul of a poet, and the mind of a man of business of the first order, that is the combination which may make a man dangerous to the world.

I think that it may have been his purpose— for he never did anything without a purpose—to give me an object-lesson of his own capacity for governing, with the idea, perhaps, that I might in turn influence others of the Émigrés by what I told them. At any rate he left me there to stand and to watch the curious succession of points upon which he had to give an opinion during a few hours. Nothing seemed to be either too large or too small for that extraordinary mind. At one instant it was the arrangements for the winter cantonments of two hundred thousand men, at the next he was discussing with de Caulaincourt the curtailing of the expenses of the household, and the possibility of suppressing some of the carriages.

'It is my desire to be economical at home so as to make a good show abroad,' said he. 'For myself, when I had the honour to be a sub-lieutenant I found that I could live very well upon 1,200 francs a year, and it would be no hardship to me to go back to it. This extravagance of the palace must be stopped. For example, I see upon your accounts that 155 cups of coffee are drunk a day, which with sugar at 4 francs and coffee at 5 francs a pound come to 20 sous a cup. It would be better to make an allowance for coffee. The stable bills are also too high. At the present price of fodder seven or eight francs a week should be enough for each horse in a stable of two hundred. I will not have any waste at the Tuileries.'

Thus within a few minutes he would pass from a question of milliards to a question of sous, and from the management of a empire to that of a stable. From time to time I could observe that he threw a little oblique glance at me as if to ask what I thought of it all, and at the time I wondered very much why my approval should be of any consequence to him. But now, when I look back and see that my following his fortunes brought over so many others of the young nobility, I understand that he saw very much further than I did.

'Well, Monsieur de Laval,' said he suddenly, 'you have seen something of my methods. Are you prepared to enter my service?'

'Assuredly, Sire,' I answered.

'I can be a very hard master when I like,' said he smiling. 'You were there when I spoke to Admiral Bruix. We have all our duty to do, and discipline is as necessary in the highest as in the lowest ranks. But anger with me never rises above here,' and he drew his hand across his throat. 'I never permit it to cloud my brain. Dr. Corvisart here would tell you that I have the slowest pulse of all his patients.'

'And that you are the fastest eater, Sire,' said a large-faced, benevolent-looking person who had been whispering to Marshal Berthier.

'Ohé, you rascal, you rake that up against me,

do you? The Doctor will not forgive me because I tell him when I am unwell that I had rather die of the disease than of the remedies. If I eat too fast it is the fault of the State, which does not allow me more than a few minutes for my meals. Which reminds me that it must be rather after my dinner hour, Constant?'

'It is four hours after it, Sire.'

'Serve it up then at once.'

'Yes, Sire. Monsieur Isabey is outside, Sire, with his dolls.'

'Ah, we shall see them at once. Show him in.'

A man entered who had evidently just arrived from a long journey. Under his arm he carried a large flat wickerwork basket.

'It is two days since I sent for you, Monsieur Isabey.'

'The courier arrived yesterday, Sire. I have been travelling from Paris ever since.'

'Have you the models there?'

'Yes, Sire.'

'Then you may lay them out on that table.'

I could not at first imagine what it meant when I saw, upon Isabey opening his basket, that

it was crammed with little puppets about a foot
high, all of them dressed in the most gorgeous silk
and velvet costumes, with trimmings of ermine
and hangings of gold lace. But presently, as the
designer took them out one by one and placed
them on the table, I understood that the Emperor,
with his extraordinary passion for detail and for
directly controlling everything in his Court, had
had these dolls dressed in order to judge the effect
of the gorgeous costumes which had been ordered
for his grand functionaries upon State occasions.

'What is this?' he asked, holding up a little
lady in hunting costume of amaranth and 'gold
with a toque and plume of white feathers.

'That is for the Empress's hunt, Sire.'

'You should have the waist rather lower,' said
Napoleon, who had very definite opinions about
ladies' dresses. 'These cursed fashions seem to
be the only thing in my dominions which I cannot
regulate. My tailor, Duchesne, takes three inches
from my coat-tails, and all the armies and fleets
of France cannot prevent him. Who is this?'

He had picked up a very gorgeous figure in a
green coat.

'That is the grand master of the hunt, Sire.'

'Then it is you, Berthier. How do you like your new costume? And this in red?'

'That is the Arch-Chancellor.'

'And the violet?'

'That is the Grand Chamberlain.'

The Emperor was as much amused as a child with a new toy. He formed little groups of the figures upon the table, so that he might have an idea of how the dignitaries would look when they chatted together. Then he threw them all back into the basket.

'Very good,' said he. 'You and David have done your work very well, Isabey. You will submit these designs to the Court outfitters and have an estimate for the expense. You may tell Lenormand that if she ventures to send in such an account as the last which she sent to the Empress she shall see the inside of Vincennes. You would not think it right, Monsieur de Laval, to spend twenty-five thousand francs upon a single dress, even though it were for Mademoiselle Eugénie de Choiseul.'

Was there anything which this wizard of a man

did not know? What could my love affairs be to
him amidst the clash of armies and the struggles
of nations? When I looked at him, half in amazement and half in fear, that pleasant boyish smile
lit up his pale face, and his plump little hand
rested for an instant upon my shoulder. His eyes
were of a bright blue when he was amused, though
they would turn dark when he was thoughtful,
and steel-grey in moments of excitement.

'You were surprised when I told you a little
while ago about your encounter with the Englishman in the village inn. You are still more surprised now when I tell you about a certain young
lady. You must certainly have thought that I was
very badly served by my agents in England if I
did not know such important details as these.'

'I cannot conceive, Sire, why such trifles should
be reported to you, or why you should for one
instant remember them.'

'You are certainly a very modest young man,
and I hope you will not lose that charming quality
when you have been for a little time at my Court.
So you think that your own private affairs are of
no importance to me?'

'I do not know why they should be, Sire.'

'What is the name of your great-uncle?'

'He is the Cardinal de Laval de Montmorency.'

'Precisely. And where is he?'

'He is in Germany.'

'Quite so—in Germany, and not at Notre Dame, where I should have placed him. Who is your first cousin?'

'The Duke de Rohan.'

'And where is he?'

'In London.'

'Yes, in London, and not at the Tuileries, where he might have had what he liked for the asking. I wonder if I were to fall whether I should have followers as faithful as those of the Bourbons. Would the men that I have made go into exile and refuse all offers until I should return? Come here, Berthier!' he took his favourite by the ear with the caressing gesture which was peculiar to him. 'Could I count upon you, you rascal—eh?'

'I do not understand you, Sire.' Our conversation had been carried on in a voice which had made it inaudible to the other people in the room,

but now they were all listening to what Berthier
had to say.

'If I were driven out, would you go into exile
also?'

'No, Sire.'

'Diable! At least you are frank.'

'I could not go into exile, Sire.'

'And why?'

'Because I should be dead, Sire.'

Napoleon began to laugh.

'And there are some who say that our
Berthier is dull-witted,' said he. 'Well, I think
I am pretty sure of you, Berthier, for although I
am fond of you for reasons of my own I do not
think that you would be of much value to anyone
else. Now I could not say that of you, Monsieur
Talleyrand. You would change very quickly to a
new master as you have changed from an old one.
You have a genius, you know, for adapting yourself.'

There was nothing which the Emperor loved
more than to suddenly produce little scenes of this
sort which made everybody very uncomfortable,
for no one could tell what awkward or compro-

mising question he was going to put to them next. At present, however, they all forgot their own fears of what might come in their interest at the reply which the famous diplomatist might make to a suggestion which everybody knew to be so true. He stood, leaning upon his black ebony stick, with his bulky shoulders stooping forward, and an amused smile upon his face, as if the most innocent of compliments had been addressed to him. One of his few titles to respect is that he always met Napoleon upon equal terms, and never condescended to fawn upon him or to flatter him.

'You think I should desert you, Sire, if your enemies offered me more than you have given me?'

'I am perfectly sure that you would.'

'Well, really I cannot answer for myself, Sire, until the offer has been made. But it will have to be a very large one. You see, apart from my very nice hotel in the Rue St. Florentin, and the two hundred thousand or so which you are pleased to allow me, there is my position as the first minister in Europe. Really, Sire, unless they put me on the throne I cannot see how I can better my position.'

'No, I think I have you pretty safe,' said Napoleon, looking hard at him with thoughtful eyes. 'By the way, Talleyrand, you must either marry Madame Grand or get rid of her, for I cannot have a scandal about the Court.'

I was astounded to hear so delicate and personal a matter discussed in this public way, but this also was characteristic of the rule of this extraordinary man, who proclaimed that he looked upon delicacy and good taste as two of the fetters with which mediocrity attempted to cripple genius. There was no question of private life, from the choosing of a wife to the discarding of a mistress, that this young conqueror of thirty-six did not claim the right of discussing and of finally settling. Talleyrand broke once more into his benevolent but inscrutable smile.

'I suppose that it is from early association, Sire,' said he, 'but my instincts are to avoid marriage.'

Napoleon began to laugh.

'I forget sometimes that it is really the Bishop

of Autun to whom I am speaking,' said he. 'I
think that perhaps I have interest enough with the
Pope to ask him, in return for any little attention
which we gave him at the Coronation, to show you
some leniency in this matter. She is a clever
woman, this Madame Grand. I have observed
that she listens with attention.'

Talleyrand shrugged his rounded shoulders.

'Intellect in a woman is not always an advantage, Sire. A clever woman compromises her
husband. A stupid woman only compromises
herself.'

'The cleverest woman,' said Napoleon, 'is the
woman who is clever enough to conceal her cleverness. The women in France have always been a
danger, for they are cleverer than the men. They
cannot understand that it is their hearts and not
their heads that we want. When they have had
influence upon a monarch, they have invariably
ruined his career. Look at Henry the Fourth and
Louis the Fourteenth. They are all ideologists,
dreamers, sentimentalists, full of emotion and
energy, but without logic or foresight. Look at that
accursed Madame de Staël! Look at the Salons

of the Quartier St. Germain! Their eternal clack, clack, clack give me more trouble than the fleet of England. Why cannot they look after their babies and their needlework? I suppose you think that these are very dreadful opinions, Monsieur de Laval?'

It was not an easy question to answer, so I was silent.

'You have not at your age become a practical man,' said the Emperor. 'You will understand then. I dare say that I thought as you do at the time when the stupid Parisians were saying what a misalliance the widow of the famous General de Beauharnais was making by marrying the unknown Buonaparte. It was a beautiful dream! There are nine inns in a single day's journey between Milan and Mantua, and I wrote a letter to my wife from each of them. Nine letters in a day—but one becomes disillusioned, monsieur. One learns to accept things as they are.'

I could not but think what a beautiful young man he must have been before he had learned to accept things as they are. The glamour, the romance—what a bald dead thing is life without it!

o

His own face had clouded over as if that old life had
perhaps had a charm which the Emperor's crown
had never given. It may be that those nine letters
written in one day at wayside inns had brought
him more true joy than all the treaties by which
he had torn provinces from his neighbours. But
the sentiment passed from his face, and he came
back in his sudden concise fashion to my own
affairs.

'Eugénie de Choiseul is the niece of the Duc
de Choiseul, is she not?' he asked.

'Yes, Sire.'

'You are affianced!'

'Yes, Sire.'

He shook his head impatiently.

'If you wish to advance yourself in my Court,
Monsieur de Laval,' said he, 'you must commit such
matters to my care. Is it likely that I can look
with indifference upon a marriage between émigrés
—an alliance between my enemies?'

'But she shares my opinions, Sire.'

'Ta, ta, ta, at her age one has no opinions.
She has the émigré blood in her veins, and it will
come out. Your marriage shall be my care,

Monsieur de Laval. And I wish you to come to the Pont de Briques that you may be presented to the Empress. What is it, Constant?'

'There is a lady outside who desires to see your Majesty. Shall I tell her to come later?'

'A lady!' cried the Emperor smiling. 'We do not see many faces in the camp which have not a moustache upon them. Who is she? What does she want?'

'Her name, Sire, is Mademoiselle Sibylle Bernac.'

'What!' cried Napoleon. It must be the daughter of old Bernac of Grosbois. By the way, Monsieur de Laval, he is your uncle upon your mother's side, is he not?'

I may have flushed with shame as I acknowledged it, for the Emperor read my feelings.

'Well, well, he has not a very savoury trade, it is true, and yet I can assure you that it is one which is very necessary to me. By the way, this uncle of yours, as I understand, holds the estates which should have descended to you, does he not?'

'Yes, Sire.'

His blue eyes flashed suspicion at me.

'I trust that you are not joining my service merely in the hope of having them restored to you.'

'No, Sire. It is my ambition to make a career for myself.'

'It is a prouder thing,' said the Emperor, 'to found a family than merely to perpetuate one. I could not restore your estates, Monsieur de Laval, for things have come to such a pitch in France that if one once begins restorations the affair is endless. It would shake all public confidence. I have no more devoted adherents than the men who hold land which does not belong to them. As long as they serve me, as your uncle serves me, the land must remain with them. But what can this young lady require of me? Show her in, Constant!'

An instant later my cousin Sibylle was conducted into the room. Her face was pale and set, but her large dark eyes were filled with resolution, and she carried herself like a princess.

'Well, mademoiselle, why do you come here? What is it that you want?' asked the Emperor in the brusque manner which he adopted to women, even if he were wooing them.

Sibylle glanced round, and as our eyes met for an instant I felt that my presence had renewed her courage. She looked bravely at the Emperor as she answered him.

'I come, Sire, to implore a favour of you.'

'Your father's daughter has certainly claims upon me, mademoiselle. What is it that you wish?'

'I do not ask it in my father's name, but in my own. I implore you, Sire, to spare the life of Monsieur Lucien Lesage, who was arrested yesterday upon a charge of treason. He is a student, Sire—a mere dreamer who has lived away from the world and has been made a tool by designing men.'

'A dreamer!' cried the Emperor harshly. 'They are the most dangerous of all.' He took a bundle of notes from his table and glanced them over. 'I presume that he is fortunate enough to be your lover, mademoiselle?'

Sibylle's pale face flushed, and she looked down before the Emperor's keen sardonic glance.

'I have his examination here. He does not come well out of it. I confess that from what I see of the young man's character I should not say that he is worthy of your love.'

'I implore you to spare him, Sire.'

'What you ask is impossible, mademoiselle. I have been conspired against from two sides—by the Bourbons and by the Jacobins. Hitherto I have been too long-suffering, and they have been encouraged by my patience. Since Cadoudal and the Duc d'Enghien died the Bourbons have been quiet. Now I must teach the same lesson to these others.'

I was astonished and am still astonished at the passion with which my brave and pure cousin loved this cowardly and low-minded man, though it is but in accordance with that strange law which draws the extremes of nature together. As she heard the Emperor's stern reply the last sign of colour faded from her pale face, and her eyes were dimmed with despairing tears, which gleamed upon her white cheeks like dew upon the petals of a lily.

'For God's sake, Sire! For the love of your mother spare him!' she cried, falling upon her knees at the Emperor's feet. 'I will answer for him that he never offends you again.'

'Tut, tut!' cried Napoleon angrily, turning

upon his heel and walking impatiently up and down the room. 'I cannot grant you what you ask, mademoiselle. When I say so once it is finished. I cannot have my decisions in high matters of State affected by the intrusion of women. The Jacobins have been dangerous of late, and an example must be made or we shall have the Faubourg St. Antoine upon our hands once more.'

The Emperor's set face and firm manner showed it was hopeless, and yet my cousin persevered as no one but a woman who pleads for her lover would have dared to do.

'He is harmless, sire.'

'His death will frighten others.'

'Spare him and I will answer for his loyalty.'

'What you ask is impossible.'

Constant and I raised her from the ground.

'That is right, Monsieur de Laval,' said the Emperor. 'This interview can lead to nothing. Remove your cousin from the room!'

But she had again turned to him with a face which showed that even now all hope had not been abandoned.

'Sire,' she cried. 'You say that an example must be made. There is Toussac——!'

'Ah, if I could lay my hands upon Toussac!'

'He is the dangerous man. It was he and my father who led Lucien on. If an example must be made it should be an example of the guilty rather than of the innocent.'

'They are both guilty. And, besides, we have our hands upon the one but not upon the other.'

'But if I could find him?'

Napoleon thought for a moment.

'If you do,' said he, 'Lesage will be forgiven!'

'But I cannot do it in a day.'

'How long do you ask?'

'A week at the least.'

'Then he has a respite of a week. If you can find Toussac in the time, Lesage will be pardoned. If not he will die upon the eighth day. It is enough. Monsieur de Laval, remove your cousin, for I have matters of more importance to attend to. I shall expect you one evening at the Pont de Briques, when you are ready to be presented to the Empress.'

"SIRE!" SHE CRIED, "YOU SAY THAT AN EXAMPLE MUST BE MADE.
THERE IS TOUSSAC'

CHAPTER XIII

THE MAN OF DREAMS

WHEN I had escorted my cousin Sibylle from the presence of the Emperor, I was surprised to find the same young hussar officer waiting outside who had commanded the guard which had brought me to the camp.

'Well, mademoiselle, what luck?' he asked excitedly, clanking towards us.

For answer Sibylle shook her head.

'Ah, I feared as much, for the Emperor is a terrible man. It was brave, indeed, of you to attempt it. I had rather charge an unshaken square upon a spent horse than ask him for anything. But my heart is heavy, mademoiselle, that you should have been unsuccessful.' His boyish blue eyes filled with tears and his fair moustache drooped in such a deplorable fashion, that I could have laughed had the matter been less serious.

'Lieutenant Gérard chanced to meet me, and escorted me through the camp,' said my cousin. 'He has been kind enough to give me sympathy in my trouble.'

'And so do I, Sibylle,' I cried; 'you carried yourself like an angel, and it is a lucky man who is blessed with your love. I trust that he may be worthy of it.'

She turned cold and proud in an instant when anyone threw a doubt upon this wretched lover of hers.

'I know him as neither the Emperor nor you can do,' said she. 'He has the heart and soul of a poet, and he is too high-minded to suspect the intrigues to which he has fallen a victim. But as to Toussac, I should have no pity upon him, for I know him to be a murderer five times over, and I know also that there will be no peace in France until he has been taken. Cousin Louis, will you help me to do it?'

The lieutenant had been tugging at his moustache and looking me up and down with a jealous eye.

'Surely, mademoiselle, you will permit me to help you?' he cried in a piteous voice.

'I may need you both,' said she. 'I will come to you if I do. Now I will ask you to ride with me to the edge of the camp and there to leave me.'

She had a quick imperative way which came charmingly from those sweet womanly lips. The grey horse upon which I had come to the camp was waiting beside that of the hussar, so we were soon in the saddle. When we were clear of the huts my cousin turned to us.

'I had rather go alone now,' said she. 'It is understood, then, that I can rely upon you.'

'Entirely,' said I.

'To the death,' cried Gérard.

'It is everything to me to have two brave men at my back,' said she, and so, with a smile, gave her horse its head and cantered off over the down-land in the direction of Grosbois.

For my part I remained in thought for some time, wondering what plan she could have in her head by which she hoped to get upon the track of Toussac. A woman's wit, spurred by the danger of her lover, might perhaps succeed where Fouché and Savary had failed. When at last I turned my horse I found my young hussar still staring after the distant rider.

'My faith! There is the woman for you, Étienne!' he kept repeating. 'What an eye! What a smile! What a rider! And she is not afraid of the Emperor. Oh, Étienne, here is the woman who is worthy of you!'

These were the little sentences which he kept muttering to himself until she vanished over the hill, when he became conscious at last of my presence.

'You are mademoiselle's cousin?' he asked. 'You are joined with me in doing something for her. I do not yet know what it is, but I am perfectly ready to do it.'

'It is to capture Toussac.'

'Excellent!'

'In order to save the life of her lover.'

There was a struggle in the face of the young hussar, but his more generous nature won.

'Sapristi! I will do even that if it will make her the happier!' he cried, and he shook the hand

which I extended towards him. 'The Hussars of
Berchény are quartered over yonder, where you see
the lines of picketed horses. If you will send for
Lieutenant Étienne Gérard you will find a sure
blade always at your disposal. Let me hear from
you then, and the sooner the better!' He shook
his bridle and was off, with youth and gallantry in
every line of him, from his red toupet and flowing
dolman to the spur which twinkled on his heel.

But for four long days no word came from my
cousin as to her quest, nor did I hear from this
grim uncle of mine at the Castle of Grosbois. For
myself I had gone into the town of Boulogne and
had hired such a room as my thin purse could
afford over the shop of a baker named Vidal, next
to the Church of St. Augustin, in the Rue des
Vents. Only last year I went back there under
that strange impulse which leads the old to tread
once more with dragging feet the same spots which
have sounded to the crisp tread of their youth.
The room is still there, the very pictures and the
plaster head of Jean Bart which used to stand upon
the side table. As I stood with my back to the
narrow window, I had around me every smallest

detail upon which my young eyes had looked ; nor
was I conscious that my own heart and feelings
had undergone much change.   And yet there, in
the little round glass which faced me, was the long
drawn, weary face of an aged man, and out of the
window, when I turned, were the bare and lonely
downs which had been peopled by that mighty host
of a hundred and fifty thousand men.   To think
that the Grand Army should have vanished away
like a shredding cloud upon a windy day, and yet
that every sordid detail of a bourgeois lodging
should remain unchanged !   Truly, if man is not
humble it is not for want of having his lesson
taught to him by Nature.

My first care after I had chosen my room was
to send to Grosbois for that poor little bundle which
I had carried ashore with me that squally night
from the English lugger.   My next was to use the
credit which my favourable reception by the
Emperor and his assurance of employment had
given me in order to obtain such a wardrobe as
would enable me to appear without discredit among
the richly dressed courtiers and soldiers who surrounded him.   It was well known that it was his

whim that he should himself be the only plainly-
dressed man in the company, and that in the most
luxurious times of the Bourbons there was never a
period when fine linen and a brave coat were more
necessary for a man who would keep in favour. A
new court and a young empire cannot afford to
take anything for granted.

It was upon the morning of the fifth day that
I received a message from Duroc, who was the
head of the household, that I was to attend the
Emperor at the headquarters in the camp, and
that a seat in one of the Imperial carriages would
be at my disposal that I might proceed with the
Court to Pont de Briques, there to be present at
the reception of the Empress. When I arrived I
was shown at once through the large entrance tent,
and admitted by Constant into the room beyond,
where the Emperor stood with his back to the
fire, kicking his heels against the grate. Talleyrand and Berthier were in attendance, and de
Meneval, the secretary, sat at the writing-table.

'Ah, Monsieur de Laval,' said the Emperor
with a friendly nod. 'Have you heard anything
yet of your charming cousin ? '

'Nothing, Sire,' I answered.

'I fear that her efforts will be in vain. I wish her every success, for we have no reason at all to fear this miserable poet, while the other is formidable. All the same, an example of some sort must be made.'

The darkness was drawing in, and Constant had appeared with a taper to light the candles, but the Emperor ordered him out.

'I like the twilight,' said he. 'No doubt, Monsieur de Laval, after your long residence in England you find yourself also most at home in a dim light. I think that the brains of these people must be as dense as their fogs, to judge by the nonsense which they write in their accursed papers.' With one of those convulsive gestures which accompanied his sudden outbursts of passion he seized a sheaf of late London papers from the table, and ground them into the fire with his heel. 'An editor!' he cried in the guttural rasping voice which I had heard when I first met him. 'What is he? A dirty man with a pen in a back office. And he will talk like one of the great Powers of Europe. I have had enough of this freedom of the

Press. There are some who would like to see it established in Paris. You are among them, Talleyrand. For my part I see no need for any paper at all except the *Moniteur* by which the Government may make known its decisions to the people.'

'I am of opinion, Sire,' said the minister, 'that it is better to have open foes than secret ones, and that it is less dangerous to shed ink than blood. What matter if your enemies have leave to rave in a few Paris papers, as long as you are at the head of five hundred thousand armed men?'

'Ta, ta, ta!' cried the Emperor impatiently. 'You speak as if I had received my crown from my father the late king. But even if I had, it would be intolerable, this government by newspaper. The Bourbons allowed themselves to be criticised, and where are they now? Had they used their Swiss Guards as I did the Grenadiers upon the eighteenth Brumaire what would have become of their precious National Assembly? There was a time when a bayonet in the stomach of Mirabeau might have settled the whole matter. Later it

P

took the heads of a king and queen and the blood of a hundred thousand people.'

He sat down, and stretched his plump, white-clad legs towards the fire. Through the blackened shreds of the English papers the red glow beat upwards upon the beautiful, pallid, sphinx-like face —the face of a poet, of a philosopher—of anything rather than of a ruthless and ambitious soldier. I have heard folk remark that no two portraits of the Emperor are alike, and the fault does not lie with the artists but with the fact that every vary-ing mood made him a different man. But in his prime, before his features became heavy, I, who have seen sixty years of mankind, can say that in repose I have never looked upon a more beautiful face.

'You have no dreams and no illusions, Talley-rand,' said he. 'You are always practical, cold, and cynical. But with me, when I am in the twi-light, as now, or when I hear the sound of the sea, my imagination begins to work. It is the same when I hear some music—especially music which repeats itself again and again like some pieces of Passaniello. They have a strange effect upon me, and I begin to Ossianise. I get large ideas and

great aspirations. It is at such times that my
mind always turns to the East, that swarming ant-
heap of the human race, where alone it is possible
to be very great. I renew my dreams of '98. I
think of the possibility of drilling and arming
these vast masses of men, and of precipitating
them upon Europe. Had I conquered Syria I
should have done this, and the fate of the world
was really decided at the siege of Acre. With
Egypt at my feet I already pictured myself
approaching India, mounted upon an elephant,
and holding in my hand a new version of the
Koran which I had myself composed. I have been
born too late. To be accepted as a world's conqueror one must claim to be divine. Alexander
declared himself to be the son of Jupiter, and no
one questioned it. But the world has grown old,
and has lost its enthusiasms. What would happen
if I were to make the same claim? Monsieur de
Talleyrand would smile behind his hand, and the
Parisians would write little lampoons upon the
walls.'

He did not appear to be addressing us, but
rather to be expressing his thoughts aloud, while

allowing them to run to the most fantastic and
extravagant lengths. This it was which he called
Ossianising, because it recalled to him the wild
vague dreams of the Gaelic Ossian, whose poems
had always had a fascination for him.   De
Meneval has told me that for an hour at a time he
has sometimes talked in this strain of the most
intimate thoughts and aspirations of his heart,
while his courtiers have stood round in silence
waiting for the instant when he would return once
more to his practical and incisive self.

'The great ruler,' said he, 'must have the
power of religion behind him as well as the power
of the sword. It is more important to command
the souls than the bodies of men. The Sultan,
for example, is the head of the faith as well as of
the army. So were some of the Roman Emperors.
My position must be incomplete until this is
accomplished. At the present instant there are
thirty departments in France where the Pope is
more powerful than I am. It is only by universal
dominion that peace can be assured in the world.
When there is only one authority in Europe,
seated at Paris, and when all the kings are so

many lieutenants who hold their crowns from the central power of France, it is then that the reign of peace will be established. Many powers of equal strength must always lead to struggles until one becomes predominant. Her central position, her wealth and her history, all mark France out as being the power which will control and regulate the others. Germany is divided. Russia is barbarous. England is insular. France only remains.'

I began to understand as I listened to him that my friends in England had not been so far wrong when they had declared that as long as he lived—this little thirty-six year old artilleryman—there could not possibly be any peace in the world. He drank some coffee which Constant had placed upon the small round table at his elbow. Then he leaned back in his chair once more, still staring moodily at the red glow of the fire, with his chin sunk upon his chest.

'In those days,' said he, 'the kings of Europe will walk behind the Emperor of France in order to hold up his train at his coronation. Each of them will have to maintain a palace in Paris, and

the city will stretch as far as Versailles. These
are the plans which I have made for Paris if she
will show herself to be worthy of them. But I
have no love for them, these Parisians, and they
have none for me, for they cannot forget that I
turned my guns upon them once before, and they
know that I am ready to do so again. I have
made them admire me and fear me, but I have
never made them like me. Look what I have done
for them. Where are the treasures of Genoa, the
pictures and statues of Venice and of the Vatican ?
They are in the Louvre. The spoils of my victories
have gone to decorate her. But they must always
be changing, always chattering. They wave their
hats at me now, but they would soon be waving
their fists if I did not give them something to talk
over and to wonder at. When other things are
quiet, I have the dome of the Invalides regilded to
keep their thoughts from mischief. Louis XIV.
gave them wars. Louis XV. gave them the
gallantries and scandals of his Court. Louis XVI.
gave them nothing, so they cut off his head. It
was you who helped to bring him to the scaffold,
Talleyrand.'

'No, Sire, I was always a moderate.'

'At least, you did not regret his death.'

'The less so, since it has made room for you, Sire.'

'Nothing could have held me down, Talleyrand. I was born to reach the highest. It has always been the same with me. I remember when we were arranging the Treaty of Campo Formio —I a young general under thirty—there was a high vacant throne with the Imperial arms in the Commissioner's tent. I instantly sprang up the steps, and threw myself down upon it. I could not endure to think that there was anything above myself. And all the time I knew in my heart all that was going to happen to me. Even in the days when my brother Lucien and I lived in a little room upon a few francs a week, I knew perfectly well that the day would come when I should stand where I am now. And yet I had no prospects and no reason for any great hopes. I was not clever at school. I was only the forty-second out of fifty-eight. At mathematics I had perhaps some ability, but at nothing else. The truth is that I was always dreaming when the others were working.

There was nothing to encourage my ambition, for the only thing which I inherited from my father was a weak stomach. Once, when I was very young, I went up to Paris with my father and my sister Caroline. We were in the Rue Richelieu, and we saw the king pass in his carriage. Who would have thought that the little boy from Corsica, who took his hat off and stared, was destined to be the next monarch of France? And yet even then I felt as if that carriage ought to belong to me. What is it, Constant?'

The discreet valet bent down and whispered something to the Emperor.

'Ah, of course,' said he. 'It was an appointment. I had forgotten it. Is she there?'

'Yes, Sire.'

'In the side room?'

'Yes, Sire.'

Talleyrand and Berthier exchanged glances, and the minister began to move towards the door.

'No, no, you can remain here,' said the Emperor. 'Light the lamps, Constant, and have the carriages ready in half-an-hour. Look over this draft of a letter to the Emperor of Austria, and let me have your observations upon it, Talley-rand. De Meneval, there is a lengthy report here as to the new dockyard at Brest. Extract what is essential from it, and leave it upon my desk at five o'clock to-morrow morning. Berthier, I will have the whole army into the boats at seven. We will see if they can embark within three hours. Monsieur de Laval, you will wait here until we start for Pont de Briques.' So with a crisp order to each of us, he walked with little swift steps across the room, and I saw his square green back and white legs framed for an instant in the door-way. There was the flutter of a pink skirt beyond, and then the curtains closed behind him.

Berthier stood biting his nails, while Talleyrand looked at him with a slight raising of his bushy eyebrows. De Meneval with a rueful face was turning over the great bundle of papers which had to be copied by morning. Constant, with a noise-less tread, was lighting the candles upon the sconces round the room.

'Which is it?' I heard the minister whisper.

'The girl from the Imperial Opera,' said Berthier.

'Is the little Spanish lady out of favour then?'

'No, I think not. She was here yesterday.'

'And the other, the Countess?'

'She has a cottage at Ambleteuse?'

'But we must have no scandal about the Court,' said Talleyrand, with a sour smile, recalling the moral sentiments with which the Emperor had reproved him. 'And now, Monsieur de Laval,' he added, drawing me aside, 'I very much wish to hear from you about the Bourbon party in England. You must have heard their views. Do they imagine that they have any chance of success?'

And so for ten minutes he plied me with questions, which showed me clearly that the Emperor had read him aright, and that he was determined, come what might, to be upon the side which won. We were still talking when Constant entered hurriedly, with a look of anxiety and perplexity which I could not have imagined upon so smooth and imperturbable a face.

'Good Heavens, Monsieur Talleyrand,' he cried,

clasping and unclasping his hands. 'Such a misfortune! Who could have expected it?'

'What is it, then, Constant?'

'Oh, Monsieur, I dare not intrude upon the
Emperor. And yet . . . And yet . . . The
Empress is outside, and she is coming in.'

CHAPTER XIV

JOSEPHINE

AT this unexpected announcement Talleyrand and Berthier looked at each other in silence, and for once the trained features of the great diplomatist, who lived behind a mask, betrayed the fact that he was still capable of emotion. The spasm which passed over them was caused, however, rather by mischievous amusement than by consternation, while Berthier—who had an honest affection for both Napoleon and Josephine—ran frantically to the door as if to bar the Empress from entering. Constant rushed towards the curtains which screened the Emperor's room, and then, losing courage, although he was known to be a stout-hearted man, he came running back to Talleyrand for advice. It was too late now, however, for Roustem the Mameluke had opened the door, and two ladies had entered the room. The first was tall and graceful, with a smiling face, and an affable though dignified manner. She was dressed in a black velvet cloak with white lace at the neck and sleeves, and she wore a black hat with a curling white feather. Her companion was shorter, with a countenance which would have been plain had it not been for the alert expression and large dark eyes, which gave it charm and character. A small black terrier dog had followed them in, but the first lady turned and handed the thin steel chain with which she led it to the Mameluke attendant.

'You had better keep Fortuné outside, Roustem,' said she, in a peculiarly sweet musical voice. 'The Emperor is not very fond of dogs, and if we intrude upon his quarters we cannot do less than consult his tastes. Good evening, Monsieur de Talleyrand! Madame de Rémusat and I have driven all along the cliffs, and we have stopped as we passed to know if the Emperor is coming to Pont de Briques. But perhaps he has already started. I had expected to find him here.'

'His Imperial Majesty was here a short time ago,' said Talleyrand, bowing and rubbing his hands.

'I hold my *salon*—such a *salon* as Pont de Briques is capable of—this evening, and the Emperor promised me that he would set his work aside for once, and favour us with his presence. I wish we could persuade him to work less, Monsieur de Talleyrand. He has a frame of iron, but he cannot continue in this way. These nervous attacks come more frequently upon him. He will insist upon doing everything, everything himself. It is noble, but it is to be a martyr. I have no doubt that at the present moment—but you have not yet told me where he is, Monsieur de Talleyrand.'

'We expect him every instant, your Majesty.'

'In that case we shall sit down and await his return. Ah, Monsieur de Meneval, how I pity you when I see you among all those papers! I was desolate when Monsieur de Bourrienne deserted the Emperor, but you have more than taken his place. Come up to the fire, Madame de Rémusat! Yes, yes, I insist upon it, for I know that you must be cold. Constant, come and put the rug under Madame de Rémusat's feet.'

It was by little acts of thoughtfulness and kind-

ness like this that the Empress so endeared herself
that she had really no enemies in France, even
among those who were most bitterly opposed to
her husband. Whether as the consort of the first
man in Europe, or as the lonely divorced woman
eating her heart out at Malmaison, she was always
praised and beloved by those who knew her. Of
all the sacrifices which the Emperor ever made to
his ambition that of his wife was the one which
cost him the greatest struggle and the keenest
regret.

Now as she sat before the fire in the same chair
which had so recently been occupied by the Emperor, I had an opportunity of studying this person,
whose strange fate had raised her from being the
daughter of a lieutenant of artillery to the first
position among the women of Europe. She was
six years older than Napoleon, and on this occasion,
when I saw her first, she was in her forty-second
year; but at a little distance or in a discreet light,
it was no courtier's flattery to say that she might
very well have passed for thirty. Her tall, elegant
figure was girlish in its supple slimness, and she
had an easy and natural grace in every movement,

which she inherited with her tropical West Indian
blood. Her features were delicate, and I have
heard that in her youth she was strikingly beautiful ;
but, like most Creole women, she had become
passée in early middle age. She had made a brave
fight, however—with art as her ally—against the
attacks of time, and her success had been such that
when she sat aloof upon a daïs or drove past in a
procession, she might still pass as a lovely woman.
In a small room, however, or in a good light, the
crude pinks and whites with which she had concealed her sallow cheeks became painfully harsh
and artificial. Her own natural beauty, however,
still lingered in that last refuge of beauty—the eyes,
which were large, dark, and sympathetic. Her
mouth, too, was small and amiable, and her most
frequent expression was a smile, which seldom
broadened into a laugh, as she had her own reasons
for preferring that her teeth should not be seen.
As to her bearing, it was so dignified, that if this
little West Indian had come straight from the loins
of Charlemagne, it could not have been improved
upon. Her walk, her glance, the sweep of her
dress, the wave of her hand—they had all the

happiest mixture of the sweetness of a woman and
the condescension of a queen. I watched her with
admiration as she leaned forward, picking little
pieces of aromatic aloes wood out of the basket and
throwing them on to the fire.

'Napoleon likes the smell of burning aloes,'
said she. 'There was never anyone who had such
a nose as he, for he can detect things which are
quite hidden from me.'

'The Emperor has an excellent nose for many
things,' said Talleyrand. 'The State contractors
have found that out to their cost.'

'Oh, it is dreadful when he comes to examine
accounts—dreadful, Monsieur de Talleyrand!
Nothing escapes him. He will make no allowances.
Everything must be exact. But who is this young
gentleman, Monsieur de Talleyrand? I do not
think that he has been presented to me.'

The minister explained in a few words that I
had been received into the Emperor's personal
service, and Josephine congratulated me upon it
with the most kindly sympathy.

'It eases my mind so to know that he has
brave and loyal men round him. Ever since that

Q

dreadful affair of the infernal machine I have always been uneasy if he is away from me. He is really safest in time of war, for it is only then that he is away from the assassins who hate him. And now I understand that a new Jacobin plot has only just been discovered.'

'This is the same Monsieur de Laval who was there when the conspirator was taken,' said Talleyrand.

The Empress overwhelmed me with questions, hardly waiting for the answers in her anxiety.

'But this dreadful man Toussac has not been taken yet,' she cried. 'Have I not heard that a young lady is endeavouring to do what has baffled the secret police, and that the freedom of her lover is to be the reward of her success?'

'She is my cousin, your Imperial Majesty. Mademoiselle Sibylle Bernac is her name.'

'You have only been in France a few days, Monsieur de Laval,' said Josephine, smiling, 'but it seems to me that all the affairs of the Empire are already revolving round you. You must bring this pretty cousin of yours—the Emperor said that she is pretty—to Court with you, and present her to me. Madame de Rémusat, you will take a note of the name.'

The Empress had stooped again to the basket of aloes wood which stood beside the fireplace. Suddenly I saw her stare hard at something, and then, with a little cry of surprise, she stooped and lifted an object from the carpet. It was the Emperor's soft flat beaver with the little tricolour cockade. Josephine sprang up, and looked from the hat in her hand to the imperturbable face of the minister.

'How is this, Monsieur de Talleyrand,' she cried, and the dark eyes began to shine with anger and suspicion. 'You said to me that the Emperor was out, and here is his hat!'

'Pardon me, your Imperial Majesty, I did not say that he was out.'

'What did you say then?'

'I said that he left the room a short time before.'

'You are endeavouring to conceal something from me,' she cried, with the quick instinct of a woman.

'I assure you that I tell you all I know.'

The Empress's eyes darted from face to face.

'Marshal Berthier,' she cried, 'I insist upon your telling me this instant where the Emperor is, and what he is doing.'

The slow-witted soldier stammered and twisted his cocked hat about.

'I know no more than Monsieur de Talleyrand does,' said he ; 'the Emperor left us some time ago.'

'By which door ?

Poor Berthier was more confused than ever.

'Really, your Imperial Majesty, I cannot undertake to say by which door it was that the Emperor quitted the apartment.'

Josephine's eyes flashed round at me, and my heart shrunk within me as I thought that she was about to ask me that same dreadful question. But I had just time to breathe one prayer to the good Saint Ignatius, who has always been gracious to our family, and the danger passed.

'Come, Madame de Rémusât,' said she. 'If these gentlemen will not tell us we shall very soon find out for ourselves.'

She swept with great dignity towards the curtained door, followed at the distance of a few yards by her waiting lady, whose frightened face and lagging, unwilling steps showed that she perfectly appreciated the situation. Indeed, the Emperor's open infidelities, and the public scenes to which they gave rise, were so notorious, that even in Ashford they had reached our ears. Napoleon's self-confidence and his contempt of the world had the effect of making him careless as to what was thought or said of him, while Josephine, when she was carried away by jealousy, lost all the dignity and restraint which usually marked her conduct; so between them they gave some embarrassing moments to those who were about them. Talleyrand turned away with his fingers over his lips, while Berthier, in an agony of apprehension, continued to double up and to twist the cocked hat which he held between his hands. Only Constant, the faithful valet, ventured to intervene between his mistress and the fatal door.

'If your Majesty will resume your seat I shall inform the Emperor that you are here,' said he, with two deprecating hands outstretched.

'Ah, then he *is* there!' she cried furiously. 'I

see it all! I understand it all! But I will expose
him—I will reproach him with his perfidy! Let
me pass, Constant! How dare you stand in my
way?'

'Allow me to announce you, your Majesty.'

'I shall announce myself.' With swift undula-
tions of her beautiful figure she darted past the
protesting valet, parted the curtains, threw open
the door, and vanished into the next room.

She had seemed a creature full of fire and of
spirit as, with a flush which broke through the
paint upon her cheeks, and with eyes which gleamed
with the just anger of an outraged wife, she forced
her way into her husband's presence. But she was
a woman of change and impulse, full of little squirts
of courage and corresponding reactions into cowardice. She had hardly vanished from our sight when
there was a harsh roar, like an angry beast, and
next instant Josephine came flying into the room
again, with the Emperor, inarticulate with passion,
raving at her heels. So frightened was she, that
she began to run towards the fireplace, upon which
Madame de Rémusat, who had no wish to form a
rearguard upon such an occasion, began running

also, and the two of them, like a pair of startled hens, came rustling and fluttering back to the seats which they had left. There they cowered whilst the Emperor, with a convulsed face and a torrent of camp-fire oaths, stamped and raged about the room.

'You, Constant, you!' he shouted; 'is this the way in which you serve me? Have you no sense then—no discretion? Am I never to have any privacy? Must I eternally submit to be spied upon by women? Is everyone else to have liberty, and I only to have none? As to you, Josephine, this finishes it all. I had hesitations before, but now I have none. This brings everything to an end between us.'

We would all, I am sure, have given a good deal to slip from the room—at least, my own embarrassment far exceeded my interest—but the Emperor from his lofty standpoint cared as little about our presence as if we had been so many articles of furniture. In fact, it was one of this strange man's peculiarities that it was just those delicate and personal scenes with which privacy is usually associated that he preferred to have in public, for he knew that his reproaches had an additional sting when they fell upon other ears besides those of his victim. From his wife to his groom there was not one of those who were about him who did not live in dread of being held up to ridicule and infamy before a smiling crowd, whose amusement was only tempered by the reflection that each of them might be the next to endure the same exposure.

As to Josephine, she had taken refuge in a woman's last resource, and was crying bitterly, with her graceful neck stooping towards her knees and her two hands over her face. Madame de Rémusat was weeping also, and in every pause of his hoarse scolding—for his voice was very hoarse and raucous when he was angry—there came the soft hissing and clicking of their sobs. Sometimes his fierce taunts would bring some reply from the Empress, some gentle reproof to him for his gallantries, but each remonstrance only excited him to a fresh rush of vituperation. In one of his outbursts he threw his snuff-box with a crash upon the floor as a spoiled child would hurl down its toys.

'Morality!' he cried, 'morality was not made

for me, and I was not made for morality. I am a
man apart, and I accept nobody's conditions. I
tell you always, Josephine, that these are the foolish
phrases of mediocre people who wish to fetter the
great. They do not apply to me. I will never
consent to frame my conduct by the puerile
arrangements of society.'

'Have you no feeling then?' sobbed the
Empress.

'A great man is not made for feeling. It is for
him to decide what he shall do, and then to do it
without interference from anyone. It is your place,
Josephine, to submit to all my fancies, and you
should think it quite natural that I should allow
myself some latitude.'

It was a favourite device of the Emperor's,
when he was in the wrong upon one point, to turn
the conversation round so as to get upon some
other one on which he was in the right. Having
worked off the first explosion of his passion he now
assumed the offensive, for in argument, as in war,
his instinct was always to attack.

'I have been looking over Lenormand's
accounts, Josephine,' said he. 'Are you aware how

many dresses you have had last year? You have
had a hundred and forty—no less—and many of
them cost as much as twenty-five thousand livres.
I am told that you have six hundred dresses in
your wardrobes, many of which have hardly ever
been used. Madame de Rémusat knows that what
I say is true. She cannot deny it.'

'You like me to dress well, Napoleon.'

'I will not have such monstrous extravagance.
I could have two regiments of cuirassiers, or a
fleet of frigates, with the money which you
squander upon foolish silks and furs. It might
turn the fortunes of a campaign. Then again,
Josephine, who gave you permission to order that
parure of diamonds and sapphires from Lefebvre?
The bill has been sent to me and I have refused to
pay for it. If he applies again, I shall have him
marched to prison between a file of grenadiers, and
your milliner shall accompany him there.'

The Emperor's fits of anger, although tempestuous, were never very prolonged. The curious
convulsive wriggle of one of his arms, which always
showed when he was excited, gradually died away,
and after looking for some time at the papers of

de Meneval—who had written away like an auto-
maton during all this uproar—he came across to
the fire with a smile upon his lips, and a brow from
which the shadow had departed.

'You have no excuse for extravagance, Josephine,' said he, laying his hand upon her shoulder.
'Diamonds and fine dresses are very necessary to
an ugly woman in order to make her attractive, but
you cannot need them for such a purpose. You
had no fine dresses when first I saw you in the Rue.
Chautereine, and yet there was no woman in the
world who ever attracted me so. Why will you
vex me, Josephine, and make me say things which
seem unkind? Drive back, little one, to Pont de
Briques, and see that you do not catch cold.'

'You will come to the salon, Napoleon?'
asked the Empress, whose bitterest resentment
seemed to vanish in an instant at the first kindly
touch from his hand. She still held her handkerchief before her eyes, but it was chiefly, I think,
to conceal the effect which her tears had had upon
her cheeks.

'Yes, yes, I will come. Our carriages will
follow yours. See the ladies into the berline,

Constant. Have you ordered the embarkation of the troops, Berthier? Come here, Talleyrand, for I wish to describe my views about the future of Spain and Portugal. Monsieur de Laval, you may escort the Empress to Pont de Briques, where I shall see you at the reception.'

CHAPTER XV

THE RECEPTION OF THE EMPRESS

PONT DE BRIQUES is but a small village, and this sudden arrival of the Court, which was to remain for some weeks, had crammed it with visitors. It would have been very much simpler to have come to Boulogne, where there were more suitable buildings and better accommodation, but Napoleon had named Pont de Briques, so Pont de Briques it had to be. The word impossible was not permitted amongst those who had to carry out his wishes. So an army of cooks and footmen settled upon the little place, and then there arrived the dignitaries of the new Empire, and then the ladies of the Court, and then their admirers from the camp. The Empress had a château for her accommodation. The rest quartered themselves in cottages or where they best might, and waited ardently for the moment which was to take them

back to the comforts of Versailles or Fontainebleau.

The Empress had graciously offered me a seat
in her berline, and all the way to the village,
entirely forgetful apparently of the scene through
which she passed, she chatted away, asking me a
thousand personal questions about myself and my
affairs, for a kindly curiosity in the doings of everyone around her was one of her most marked
characteristics. Especially was she interested in
Eugénie, and as the subject was one upon which I
was equally interested in talking it ended in a
rhapsody upon my part, amid little sympathetic
ejaculations from the Empress and titterings from
Madame de Rémusat.

'But you must certainly bring her over to the
Court!' cried the kindly woman. 'Such a paragon
of beauty and of virtue must not be allowed to
waste herself in this English village. Have you
spoken about her to the Emperor?'

'I found that he knew all about her, your
Majesty.'

'He knows all about everything. Oh, what a
man he is! You heard him about those diamonds

and sapphires. Lefebvre gave me his word that no one should know of it but ourselves, and that I should pay at my leisure, and yet you see that the Emperor knew. But what did he say, Monsieur de Laval?'

'He said that my marriage should be his affair.'

Josephine shook her head and groaned.

'But this is serious, Monsieur de Laval. He is capable of singling out any one of the ladies of the Court and marrying you to her within a week. It is a subject upon which he will not listen to argument. He has brought about some extraordinary matches in this way. But I will speak to the Emperor before I return to Paris, and I will see what I can arrange for you.'

I was still endeavouring to thank her for her sympathy and kindness when the berline rattled up the drive and pulled up at the entrance to the château, where the knot of scarlet footmen and the bearskins of two sentries from the Guards announced the Imperial quarters. The Empress and her lady hurried away to prepare their toilets for the evening, and I was shown at once into the salon, in which the guests had already begun to assemble.

This was a large square room furnished as modestly as the sitting-room of a provincial gentleman would be likely to be. The wall-paper was gloomy, and the furniture was of dark mahogany upholstered in faded blue nankeen, but there were numerous candles in candelabra upon the tables and in sconces upon the walls which gave an air of festivity even to these sombre surroundings. Out of the large central room were several smaller ones in which card-tables had been laid out, and the doorways between had been draped with Oriental chintz. A number of ladies and gentlemen were standing about, the former in the high evening dresses to which the Emperor had given his sanction, the latter about equally divided between the civilians in black court costumes and the soldiers in their uniforms. Bright colours and graceful draperies predominated, for in spite of his lectures about economy the Emperor was very harsh to any lady who did not dress in a manner which would sustain the brilliancy of his Court. The prevailing fashions gave an opening to taste and to display, for the simple classical costumes had died out with the Republic, and Oriental dresses had taken their place as a compliment to the Conqueror of Egypt. Lucretia had changed to Zuleika, and the salons which had reflected the austerity of old Rome had turned suddenly into so many Eastern harems.

On entering the room I had retired into a corner, fearing that I should find none there whom I knew; but someone plucked at my arm, and turning round I found myself looking into the yellow inscrutable face of my uncle Bernac. He seized my unresponsive hand and wrung it with a false cordiality.

'My dear Louis,' said he. 'It was really the hope of meeting you here which brought me over from Grosbois—although you can understand that living so far from Paris I cannot afford to miss such an opportunity of showing myself at Court. Nevertheless I can assure you that it was of you principally that I was thinking. I hear that you have had a splendid reception from the Emperor, and that you have been taken into his personal service. I had spoken to him about you, and I

R

made him fully realise that if he treats you well
he is likely to coax some of the other young
émigrés into his service.'

I was convinced that he was lying, but none
the less I had to bow and utter a few words of cold
thanks.

'I see that you still bear me some grudge for
what passed between us the other day,' said he,
'but really, my dear Louis, you have no occasion
to do so. It was your own good which I had
chiefly at heart. I am neither a young nor a
strong man, Louis, and my profession, as you
have seen, is a dangerous one. There is my child,
and there is my estate. Who takes one, takes
both. Sibylle is a charming girl, and you must
not allow yourself to be prejudiced against her by
any ill temper which she may have shown towards
me. I will confess that she had some reason to be
annoyed at the turn which things had taken. But
I hope to hear that you have now thought better
upon this matter.'

'I have never thought about it at all, and I beg
that you will not discuss it,' said I curtly.

He stood in deep thought for a few moments,

and then he raised his evil face and his cruel grey eyes to mine.

'Well, well, that is settled then,' said he. 'But you cannot bear me a grudge for having wished you to be my successor. Be reasonable, Louis. You must acknowledge that you would now be six feet deep in the salt-marsh with your neck broken if I had not stood your friend, at some risk to myself. Is that not true?'

'You had your own motive for that,' said I.

'Very likely. But none the less I saved you. Why should you bear me ill will? It is no fault of mine if I hold your estate.'

'It is not on account of that.'

'Why is it then?'

I could have explained that it was because he had betrayed his comrades, because his daughter hated him, because he had ill-used his wife, because my father regarded him as the source of all his troubles—but the salon of the Empress was no place for a family quarrel, so I merely shrugged my shoulders, and was silent.

'Well, I am very sorry,' said he, 'for I had the best of intentions towards you. I could have advanced you, for there are few men in France who exercise more influence. But I have one request to make to you.'

'What is that, sir?'

'I have a number of personal articles, belonging to your father—his sword, his seals, a deskful of letters, some silver plate—such things in short as you would wish to keep in memory of him. I should be glad if you will come to Grosbois—if it is only for one night—and look over these things, choosing what you wish to take away. My conscience will then be clear about them.'

I promised readily that I would do so.

'And when would you come?' he asked eagerly. Something in the tone of his voice aroused my suspicions, and glancing at him I saw exultation in his eyes. I remembered the warning of Sibylle.

'I cannot come until I have learned what my duties with the Emperor are to be. When that is settled I shall come.'

'Very good. Next week perhaps, or the week afterwards. I shall expect you eagerly, Louis. I rely ·upon your promise, for a Laval was never

known to break one.' With another unanswered
squeeze of my hand, he slipped off among the crowd,
which was growing denser every instant in the
salon.

I was standing in silence thinking over this
sinister invitation of my uncle's, when I heard my
own name, and, looking up, I saw de Caulaincourt,
with his brown handsome face and tall elegant
figure, making his way towards me.

'It is your first entrance at Court, is it not,
Monsieur de Laval,' said he, in his high-bred
cordial manner; 'you should not feel lonely, for
there are certainly many friends of your father
here who will be overjoyed to make the acquaintance
of your father's son. From what de Meneval told
me I gather that you know hardly anyone—even
by sight.'

'I know the Marshals,' said I; 'I saw them all
at the council in the Emperor's tent. There is
Ney with the red head. And there is Lefebvre with
his singular mouth, and Bernadotte with the beak
of a bird of prey.'

'Precisely. And that is Rapp, with the round,
bullet head. He is talking to Junot, the handsome

dark man with the whiskers. These poor soldiers are very unhappy.'

'Why so ?' I asked.

'Because they are all men who have risen from nothing. This society and etiquette terrifies them much more than all the dangers of war. When they can hear their sabres clashing against their big boots they feel at home, but when they have to stand about with their cocked hats under their arms, and have to pick their spurs out of the ladies' trains, and talk about David's picture or Passaniello's opera, it prostrates them. The Emperor will not even permit them to swear, although he has no scruples upon his own account. He tells them to be soldiers with the army, and courtiers with the Court, but the poor fellows cannot help being soldiers all the time. Look at Rapp with his twenty wounds, endeavouring to exchange little delicate drolleries with that young lady. There, you see, he has said something which would have passed very well with a vivandière, but it has made her fly to her mamma, and he is scratching his head, for he cannot imagine how he has offended her.'

'Who is the beautiful woman with the white dress and the tiara of diamonds?' I asked.

'That is Madame Murat, who is the sister of the Emperor. Caroline is beautiful, but she is not as pretty as her sister Marie, whom you see over yonder in the corner. Do you see the tall stately dark-eyed old lady with whom she is talking? That is Napoleon's mother—a wonderful woman, the source of all their strength, shrewd, brave, vigorous, forcing respect from everyone who knows her. She is as careful and as saving as when she was the wife of a small country gentleman in Corsica, and it is no secret that she has little confidence in the permanence of the present state of things, and that she is always laying by for an evil day. The Emperor does not know whether to be amused or exasperated by her precautions. Well, Murat, I suppose we shall see you riding across the Kentish hop-fields before long.'

The famous soldier had paused opposite to us, and shook hands with my companion. His elegant well-knit figure, large fiery eyes, and noble bearing made this innkeeper's boy a man who would have drawn attention and admiration to himself in any assembly in Europe. His mop of curly hair and thick red lips gave that touch of character and individuality to his appearance which redeem a handsome face from insipidity.

'I am told that it is devilish bad country for cavalry—all cut up into hedges and ditches,' said he. 'The roads are good, but the fields are impossible. I hope that we are going soon, Monsieur de Caulaincourt, for our men will all settle down as gardeners if this continues. They are learning more about watering-pots and spuds than about horses and sabres.'

'The army, I hear, is to embark to-morrow.'

'Yes, yes, but you know very well that they will disembark again upon the wrong side of the Channel. Unless Villeneuve scatters the English fleet, nothing can be attempted.'

'Constant tells me that the Emperor was whistling "Malbrook" all the time that he was dressing this morning, and that usually comes before a move.'

'It was very clever of Constant to tell what tune it was which the Emperor was whistling,' said Murat, laughing. 'For my part I do not think that he knows the difference between the " Malbrook " and the " Marseillaise." Ah, here is the Empress—and how charming she is looking ! '

Josephine had entered, with several of her ladies in her train, and the whole assembly rose to do her honour. The Empress was dressed in an evening gown of rose-coloured tulle, spangled with silver stars—an effect which might have seemed meretricious and theatrical in another woman, but which she carried off with great grace and dignity. A little sheaf of diamond wheat-ears rose above her head, and swayed gently as she walked. No one could entertain more charmingly than she, for she moved about among the people with her amiable smile, setting everybody at their ease by her kindly natural manner, and by the conviction which she gave them that she was thoroughly at her ease herself.

' How amiable she is ! ' I exclaimed. 'Who could help loving her ? '

' There is only one family which can resist her,' said de Caulaincourt, glancing round to see that Murat was out of hearing. ' Look at the faces of the Emperor's sisters.'

I was shocked when I followed his direction to
see the malignant glances with which these two
beautiful women were following the Empress as
she walked about the room.   They whispered
together and tittered maliciously.   Then Madame
Murat turned to her mother behind her, and the
stern old lady tossed her haughty head in derision
and contempt.

'They feel that Napoléon is theirs and that they
ought to have everything.   They cannot bear to
think that she is Her Imperial Majesty and they
are only Her Highness.   They all hate her, Joseph,
Lucien—all of them.   When they had to carry
her train at the coronation they tried to trip her
up, and the Emperor had to interfere.   Oh
yes, they have the real Corsican blood, and they
are not very comfortable people to get along
with.'

But in spite of the evident hatred of her husband's family, the Empress appeared to be entirely
unconcerned and at her ease as she strolled about
among the groups of her guests with a kindly
glance and a pleasant word for each of them.   A
tall, soldierly man, brown-faced and moustached,

walked beside her, and she occasionally laid her hand with a caressing motion upon his arm.

'That is her son, Eugène de Beauharnais,' said my companion.

'Her son!' I exclaimed, for he seemed to me to be the older of the two.

De Caulaincourt smiled at my surprise.

'You know she married Beauharnais when she was very young—in fact she was hardly sixteen. She has been sitting in her boudoir while her son has been baking in Egypt and Syria, so that they have pretty well bridged over the gap between them. Do you see the tall, handsome, clean-shaven man who has just kissed Josephine's hand. That is Talma the famous actor. He once helped Napoleon at a critical moment of his career, and the Emperor has never forgotten the debt which the Consul contracted. That is really the secret of Talleyrand's power. He lent Napoleon a hundred thousand francs before he set out for Egypt, and now, however much he distrusts him, the Emperor cannot forget that old kindness. I have never known him to abandon a friend or to forgive an enemy.

If you have once served him well you may do what you like afterwards. There is one of his coachmen who is drunk from morning to night. But he gained the cross at Marengo, and so he is safe.'

De Caulaincourt had moved on to speak with some lady, and I was again left to my own thoughts, which turned upon this extraordinary man, who presented himself at one moment as a hero and at another as a spoiled child, with his nobler and his worse side alternating so rapidly that I had no sooner made up my mind about him than some new revelation would destroy my views and drive me to some fresh conclusion. That he was necessary to France was evident, and that in serving him one was serving one's country. But was it an honour or a penance to serve him? Was he worthy merely of obedience, or might love and esteem be added to it? These were the questions which we found it difficult to answer—and some of us will never have answered them up to the end of time.

The company had now lost all appearance of formality, and even the soldiers seemed to be at their ease. Many had gone into the side rooms,

where they had formed tables for whist and for vingt-
et-un. For my own part I was quite entertained
by watching the people, the beautiful women, the
handsome men, the bearers of names which had
been heard of in no previous generation, but which
now rung round the world. Immediately in front
of me were Ney, Lannes, and Murat chatting together and laughing with the freedom of the camp.
Of the three, two were destined to be executed in
cold blood, and the third to die upon the battle-field,
but no coming shadow ever cast a gloom upon
their cheery, full-blooded lives.

A small, silent, middle-aged man, who looked
unhappy and ill at ease, had been leaning against
the wall beside me. Seeing that he was as great a
stranger as myself, I addressed some observation
to him, to which he replied with great good-will,
but in the most execrable French.

'You don't happen to understand English?'
he asked. 'I've never met one living soul in this
country who did.'

'Oh yes, I understand it very well, for I have
lived most of my life over yonder. But surely you
are not English, sir? I understood that every

Englishman in France was under lock and key ever since the breach of the treaty of Amiens.'

'No, I am not English,' he answered, 'I am an American. My name is Robert Fulton, and I have to come to these receptions because it is the only way in which I can keep myself in the memory of the Emperor, who is examining some inventions of mine which will make great changes in naval warfare.

Having nothing else to do I asked this curious American what his inventions might be, and his replies very soon convinced me that I had to do with a madman. He had some idea of making a ship go against the wind and against the current by means of coal or wood which was to be burned inside of her. There was some other non-sense about floating barrels full of gunpowder which would blow a ship to pieces if she struck against them. I listened to him at the time with an indulgent smile, but now looking back from the point of vantage of my old age I can see that not all the warriors and statesmen in that room—no, not even the Emperor himself—have had as great an effect upon the history of the world as that silent American who looked so drab and so commonplace among the gold-slashed uniforms and the Oriental dresses.

-But suddenly our conversation was interrupted by a hush in the room—such a cold, uncomfortable hush as comes over a roomful of happy, romping children when a grave-faced elder comes amongst them. The chatting and the laughter died away. The sound of the rustling cards and of the clicking counters had ceased in the other rooms. Everyone, men and women, had risen to their feet with a constrained expectant expression upon their faces. And there in the doorway were the pale face and the green coat with the red cordon across the white waistcoat.

There was no saying how he might behave upon these occasions. Sometimes he was capable of being the merriest and most talkative of the company, but this was rather in his consular than in his imperial days. On the other hand he might be absolutely ferocious, with an insulting observation for everyone with whom he came in contact. As a rule he was between these two extremes, silent, morose, ill at ease, shooting out curt little remarks which made everyone uncomfortable. There was always a sigh of relief when he would pass from one room into the next.

On this occasion he seemed to have not wholly recovered from the storm of the afternoon, and he looked about him with a brooding eye and a lowering brow. It chanced that I was not very far from the door, and that his glance fell upon me.

'Come here, Monsieur de Laval,' said he. He laid his hand upon my shoulder and turned to a big, gaunt man who had accompanied him into the room. 'Look here, Cambacérès, you simpleton,' said he. 'You always said that the old families would never come back, and that they would settle in England as the Huguenots have done. You see that, as usual, you have miscalculated, for here is the heir of the de Lavals come to offer his services. Monsieur de Laval, you are now my aide-de-camp, and I beg you to keep with me wherever I go.'

This was promotion indeed, and yet I had sense enough to know that it was not for my own sweet sake that the Emperor had done it, but in order to encourage others to follow me. My conscience approved what I had done, for no sordid motive and nothing but the love of my country had prompted me; but now, as I walked round behind Napoleon, I felt humiliated and ashamed, like a prisoner led behind the car of his captor.

And soon there was something else to make me ashamed, and that was the conduct of him whose servant I had become. His manners were outrageous. As he had himself said, it was his nature to be always first, and this being so he resented those courtesies and gallantries by which men are accustomed to disguise from women the fact that they are the weaker sex. The Emperor, unlike Louis XIV., felt that even a temporary and conventional attitude of humility towards a woman was too great a condescension from his own absolute supremacy. Chivalry was among those conditions of society which he refused to accept.

To the soldiers he was amiable enough, with a nod and a joke for each of them. To his sisters also he said a few words, though rather in the tone of a drill sergeant to a pair of recruits. It was only when the Empress had joined him that his ill-humour came to a head.

'I wish you would not wear those wisps of pink about your head, Josephine,' said he, pettishly. 'All that women have to think about is how to dress themselves, and yet they cannot even do that with moderation or taste. If I see you again in such a thing I will thrust it in the fire as I did your shawl the other day.'

'You are so hard to please, Napoleon. You like one day what you cannot abide the next. But I will certainly change it if it offends you,' said Josephine, with admirable patience.

The Emperor took a few steps between the people, who had formed a lane for us to pass through. Then he stopped and looked over his shoulder at the Empress.

'How often have I told you, Josephine, that I cannot tolerate fat women.'

'I always bear it in mind, Napoleon.'

'Then why is Madame de Chevreux present?'

'But surely, Napoleon, madame is not very fat.'

'She is fatter than she should be. I should prefer not to see her. Who is this?' He had paused before a young lady in a blue dress, whose knees seemed to be giving way under her as the terrible Emperor transfixed her with his searching eyes.

'This is Mademoiselle de Bergerot.'

'How old are you?'

'Twenty-three, sire.'

'It is time that you were married. Every woman should be married at twenty-three. How is it that you are not married?'

The poor girl appeared to be incapable of answering, so the Empress gently remarked that it was to the young men that that question should be addressed.

'Oh, that is the difficulty, is it?' said the Emperor. 'We must look about and find a husband for you.' He turned, and to my horror I found his eyes fixed with a questioning gaze upon my face.

'We have to find you a wife also, Monsieur de Laval,' said he. 'Well, well, we shall see—we shall see. What is your name?' to a quiet refined man in black.

'I am Grétry, the musician.'

'Yes, yes, I remember you. I have seen you

a hundred times, but I can never recall your name. Who are you?'

'I am Joseph de Chenier.'

'Of course. I have seen your tragedy. I have forgotten the name of it, but it was not good. You have written some other poetry, have you not?'

'Yes, sire. I had your permission to dedicate my last volume to you.'

'Very likely, but I have not had time to read it. It is a pity that we have no poets now in France, for the deeds of the last few years would have given a subject for a Homer or a Virgil. It seems that I can create kingdoms but not poets. Whom do you consider to be the greatest French writer?'

'Racine, sire.'

'Then you are a blockhead, for Corneille was infinitely greater. I have no ear for metre or trivialities of the kind, but I can sympathise with the spirit of poetry, and I am conscious that Corneille is far the greatest of poets. I would have made him my prime minister had he had the good fortune to live in my epoch. It is his intellect which I admire, his knowledge of the human heart, and his profound feeling. Are you writing anything at present ? '

' I am writing a tragedy upon Henry IV., sire.'

' It will not do, sir. It is too near the present day, and I will not have politics upon the stage. Write a play about Alexander. What is your name ? '

He had pitched upon the same person whom he had already addressed.

' I am still Grétry, the musician,' said he meekly.

The Emperor flushed for an instant at the implied rebuke. He said nothing, however, but passed on to where several ladies were standing together near the door of the card-room.

' Well, madame,' said he to the nearest of them, ' I hope you are behaving rather better. When last I heard from Paris your doings were furnishing the Quartier St. Germain with a good deal of amusement and gossip.'

' I beg that your Majesty will explain what you mean,' said she with spirit.

'They had coupled your name with that of Colonel Lasalle.'

'It is a foul calumny, sire.'

'Very possibly, but it is awkward when so many calumnies cluster round one person. You are certainly a most unfortunate lady in that respect. You had a scandal once before with General Rapp's aide-de-camp. This must come to an end. What is your name?' he continued, turning to another.

'Mademoiselle de Périgord.'

'Your age?'

'Twenty.'

'You are very thin and your elbows are red. My God, Madame Boismaison, are we never to see anything but this same grey gown and the red turban with the diamond crescent?'

'I have never worn it before, sire?'

'Then you had another the same, for I am weary of the sight of it. Let me never see you in it again. Monsieur de Rémusat, I make you a good allowance. Why do you not spend it?'

'I do, sire.'

'I hear that you have been putting down your

carriage. I do not give you money to hoard in a bank, but I give it to you that you may keep up a fitting appearance with it. Let me hear that your carriage is back in the coach-house when I return to Paris. Junot, you rascal, I hear that you have been gambling and losing.'

'The most infernal run of luck, sire,' said the soldier, 'I give you my word that the ace fell four times running.'

'Ta, ta, you are a child, with no sense of the value of money. How much do you owe ? '

'Forty thousand, sire.'

'Well, well, go to Lebrun and see what he can do for you. After all, we were together at Toulon.'

'A thousand thanks, sire.'

'Tut ! You and Rapp and Lasalle are the spoiled children of the army. But no more cards, you rascal ! I do not like low dresses, Madame Picard. They spoil even pretty women, but in you they are inexcusable. Now, Josephine, I am going to my room, and you can come in half an hour and read me to sleep. I am tired to-night, but I came to your salon, since you desired that I should

help you in welcoming and entertaining your
guests. You can remain here, Monsieur de Laval,
for your presence will not be necessary until I send
you my orders.'

And so the door closed behind him, and with
a long sigh of relief from everyone, from the
Empress to the waiter with the negus, the friendly
chatter began once more, with the click of the
counters and the rustle of the cards just as
they had been before he came to help in the
entertainment.

CHAPTER XVI

THE LIBRARY OF GROSBOIS

AND now, my friends, I am coming to the end
of those singular adventures which I encountered
upon my arrival in France, adventures which
might have been of some interest in themselves
had I not introduced the figure of the Emperor,
who has eclipsed them all as completely as the
sun eclipses the stars. Even now, you see, after
all these years, in an old man's memoirs, the
Emperor is still true to his traditions, and will not
brook any opposition. As I draw his words and
his deeds I feel that my own poor story withers
before them. And yet if it had not been for
that story I should not have had an excuse for
describing to you my first and most vivid im-
pressions of him, and so it has served a purpose
after all. You must bear with me now while I tell

you of our expedition to the Red Mill and of what befell in the library of Grosbois.

Two days had passed away since the reception of the Empress Josephine, and only one remained of the time which had been allowed to my cousin Sibylle in which she might save her lover, and capture the terrible Toussac. For my own part I was not so very anxious that she should save this craven lover of hers, whose handsome face belied the poor spirit within him. And yet this lonely beautiful woman, with the strong will and the loyal heart, had touched my feelings, and I felt that I would help her to anything—even against my own better judgment, if she should desire it. It was then with a mixture of feelings that late in the afternoon I saw her and General Savary enter the little room in which I lodged at Boulogne. One glance at her flushed cheeks and triumphant eyes told me that she was confident in her own success.

'I told you that I would find him, Cousin Louis!' she cried; 'I have come straight to you, because you said that you would help in the taking of him.'

'Mademoiselle insists upon it that I should not use soldiers,' said Savary, shrugging his shoulders.

'No, no, no,' she cried with vehemence. 'It has to be done with discretion, and at the sight of a soldier he would fly to some hiding-place, where you would never be able to follow him. I cannot afford to run a risk. There is too much already at stake.'

'In such an affair three men are as useful as thirty,' said Savary. 'I should not in any case have employed more. You say that you have another friend, Lieutenant—— ? '

'Lieutenant Gérard of the Hussars of Berchény.'

'Quite so. There is not a more gallant officer in the Grand Army than Étienne Gérard. The three of us, Monsieur de Laval, should be equal to any adventure.'

'I am at your disposal.'

'Tell us then, mademoiselle, where Toussac is hiding.'

'He is hiding at the Red Mill.'

'But we have searched it, I assure you that he is not there.'

'When did you search it?' '

'Two days ago.'

'Then he has come there since. I knew that Jeanne Portal loved him. I have watched her for six days. Last night she stole down to the Red Mill with a basket of wine and fruit. All the morning I have seen her eyes sweeping the country side, and I have read the terror in them whenever she has seen the twinkle of a bayonet. I am as sure that Toussac is in the mill as if I had seen him with my own eyes.'

'In that case there is not an instant to be lost,' cried Savary. 'If he knows of a boat upon the coast he is as likely as not to slip away after dark and make his escape for England. From the Red Mill one can see all the surrounding country, and Mademoiselle is right in thinking that a large body of soldiers would only warn him to escape.'

'What do you propose then?' I asked.

'That you meet us at the south gate of the camp in an hour's time dressed as you are. You might be any gentleman travelling upon the high road. I shall see Gérard, and we shall adopt some suitable disguise. Bring your pistols, for it is with the most desperate man in France we have to do. We shall have a horse at your disposal.'

The setting sun lay dull and red upon the western horizon, and the white chalk cliffs of the French coast had all flushed into pink when I found myself once more at the gate of the Boulogne Camp. There was no sign of my companions, but a tall man, dressed in a blue coat with brass buttons like a small country farmer, was tightening the girth of a magnificent black horse, whilst a little further on a slim young ostler was waiting by the roadside, holding the bridles of two others. It was only when I recognised one of the pair as the horse which I had ridden on my first coming to camp that I answered the smile upon the keen handsome face of the ostler, and saw the swarthy features of Savary under the broad-brimmed hat of the farmer.

' I think that we may travel without fearing to excite suspicion,' said he. ' Crook that straight back of yours a little, Gérard ! And now we shall push upon our way, or we may find that we are too late.'

My life has had its share of adventures, and yet, somehow, this ride stands out above the others.

There over the waters I could dimly see the loom of the English coast, with its suggestions of dreamy villages, humming bees, and the pealing of Sunday bells. I thought of the long, white High Street of Ashford, with its red brick houses, and the inn with the great swinging sign. All my life had been spent in these peaceful surroundings, and now, here I was with a spirited horse between my knees, two pistols peeping out of my holsters, and a commission upon which my whole future might depend, to arrest the most redoubtable conspirator in France. No wonder that, looking back over many dangers and many vicissitudes, it is still that evening ride over the short crisp turf of the downs which stands out most clearly in my memory. One becomes *blasé* to adventure, as one becomes *blasé* to all else which the world can give, save only the simple joys of home, and to taste the full relish of such an expedition one must approach it with the hot blood of youth still throbbing in one's veins.

Our route, when we had left the uplands of Boulogne behind us, lay along the skirts of that desolate marsh in which I had wandered, and so inland, through plains of fern and bramble, until the

familiar black keep of the Castle of Grosbois rose
upon the left.   Then, under the guidance of Savary,
we struck to the right down a sunken road, and so
over the shoulder of a hill until, on a further slope
beyond, we saw the old windmill black against the
evening sky.   Its upper window burned red like a
spot of blood in the last rays of the setting sun.
Close by the door stood a cart full of grain sacks,
with the shafts pointing downwards and the horse
grazing at some distance.   As we gazed, a woman
appeared upon the downs and stared round, with
her hand over her eyes.

  ' See that ! ' said Savary eagerly.   ' He is there
sure enough, or why should they be on their guard ?
Let us take this road which winds round the hill,
and they will not see us until we are at the very
door.'

  ' Should we not gallop forward ? ' I suggested.

  ' The ground is too cut up.   The longer way is
the safer.   As long as we are upon the road they
cannot tell us from any other travellers.'

  We walked our horses along the path, therefore,
with as unconcerned an air as we could assume ;
but a sharp exclamation made us glance suddenly

round, and there was the woman standing on a hillock by the roadside and gazing down at us with a face that was rigid with suspicion. The sight of the military bearing of my companions changed all her fear into certainties. In an instant she had whipped the shawl from her shoulders, and was waving it frantically over her head. With a hearty curse Savary spurred his horse up the bank and galloped straight for the mill, with Gérard and myself at his heels.

It was only just in time. We were still a hundred paces from the door when a man sprang out from it, and gazed about him, his head whisking this way and that. There could be no mistaking the huge bristling beard, the broad chest, and the rounded shoulders of Toussac. A glance showed him that we would ride him down before he could get away, and he sprang back into the mill, closing the heavy door with a clang behind him.

'The window, Gérard, the window!' cried Savary.

There was a small, square window opening into the basement room of the mill. The young hussar disengaged himself from the saddle and flew through

it as the clown goes through the hoops at
Franconi's. An instant later he had opened the
door for us, with the blood streaming from his face
and hands.

'He has fled up the stair,' said he.

'Then we need be in no hurry, since he cannot
pass us,' said Savary, as we sprang from our
horses. 'You have carried his first line of
entrenchments most gallantly, Lieutenant Gérard.
I hope you are not hurt?'

'A few scratches, General, nothing more.'

'Get your pistols, then. Where is the miller?'

'Here I am,' said a squat, rough little fellow,
appearing in the open doorway. 'What do you
mean, you brigands, by entering my mill in this
fashion? I am sitting reading my paper and
smoking my pipe of coltsfoot, as my custom is
about this time of the evening, and suddenly,
without a word, a man comes flying through my
window, covers me with glass, and opens my door
to his friends outside. I've had trouble enough
with my one lodger all day without three more of
you turning up.'

T

'You have the conspirator Toussac in your house.'

'Toussac!' cried the miller. 'Nothing of the kind. His name is Maurice, and he is a merchant in silks.'

'He is the man we want. We come in the Emperor's name.'

The miller's jaw dropped as he listened.

'I don't know who he is, but he offered a good price for a bed and I asked no more questions. In these days one cannot expect a certificate of character from every lodger. But, of course, if it is a matter of State, why, it is not for me to interfere. But, to do him justice, he was a quiet gentleman enough until he had that letter just now.'

'What letter? Be careful what you say, you rascal, for your own head may find its way into the sawdust basket.'

'It was a woman who brought it. I can only tell you what I know. He has been talking like a madman ever since. It made my blood run cold to hear him. There's someone whom he swears he will murder. I shall be very glad to see the last of him.'

'Now, gentlemen,' said Savary, drawing his sword, ' we may leave our horses here. There is no window for forty feet, so he cannot escape from us. If you will see that your pistols are primed, we shall soon bring the fellow to terms.'

The stair was a narrow winding one made of wood, which led to a small loft lighted from a slit in the wall.

Some remains of wood and a litter of straw showed that this was where Toussac had spent his day. There was, however, no sign of him now, and it was evident that he had ascended the next flight of steps. We climbed them, only to find our way barred by a heavy door.

'Surrender, Toussac!' cried Savary. 'It is useless to attempt to escape us.

A hoarse laugh sounded from behind the door.

'I am not a man who surrenders. But I will make a bargain with you. I have a small matter of business to do to-night. If you will leave me alone, I will give you my solemn pledge to surrender at the camp to-morrow. I have a little debt that I wish to pay. It is only to-day that I understood to whom I owed it.'

'What you ask is impossible.'

'It would save you a great deal of trouble.'

'We cannot grant such a request. You must surrender.'

'You'll have some work first.'

'Come, come, you cannot escape us. Put your shoulders against the door! Now, all together?'

There was the hot flash of a pistol from the key-hole, and a bullet smacked against the wall between us. We hurled ourselves against the door. It was massive, but rotten with age. With a splintering and rending it gave way before us. We rushed in, weapons in hand, to find ourselves in an empty room.

'Where the devil has he got to?' cried Savary, glaring round him. 'This is the top room of all. There is nothing above it.'

It was a square empty space with a few corn-bags littered about. At the further side was an open window, and beside it lay a pistol, still smoking from the discharge. We all rushed across, and, as we craned our heads over, a simultaneous cry of astonishment escaped from us.

The distance to the ground was so great that no

WE RUSHED IN WEAPONS IN HAND, TO FIND OURSELVES IN AN EMPTY ROOM

one could have survived the fall, but Toussac had taken advantage of the presence of that cart full of grain-sacks, which I have described as having lain close to the mill. This had both shortened the distance and given him an excellent means of breaking the fall. Even so, however, the shock had been tremendous, and as we looked out he was lying panting heavily upon the top of the bags. Hearing our cry, however, he looked up, shook his fist defiantly, and, rolling from the cart, he sprang on to the back of Savary's black horse, and galloped off across the downs, his great beard flying in the wind, untouched by the pistol bullets with which we tried to bring him down.

How we flew down those creaking wooden stairs and out through the open door of the mill! Quick as we were, he had a good start, and by the time Gérard and I were in the saddle he had become a tiny man upon a small horse galloping up the green slope of the opposite hill. The shades of evening, too, were drawing in, and upon his left was the huge salt-marsh, where we should have found it difficult to follow him. The chances were certainly in his favour. And yet he never swerved from his course, but kept straight on across the downs on a line which took him farther and farther from the sea. Every instant we feared to see him dart away in the morass, but still he held his horse's head against the hill-side. What could he be making for? He never pulled rein and never glanced round, but flew onwards, like a man with a definite goal in view.

Lieutenant Gérard and I were lighter men, and our mounts were as good as his, so that it was not long before we began to gain upon him. If we could only keep him in sight it was certain that we should ride him down; but there was always the danger that he might use his knowledge of the country to throw us off his track. As we sank beneath each hill my heart sank also, to rise again with renewed hope as we caught sight of him once more galloping in front of us.

But at last that which I had feared befell us. We were not more than a couple of hundred paces behind him when we lost all trace of him. He had vanished behind some rolling ground, and we could see nothing of him when we reached the summit.

'There is a road there to the left,' cried Gérard, whose Gascon blood was aflame with excitement. 'On, my friend, on, let us keep to the left!'

'Wait a moment!' I cried. 'There is a bridle-path upon the right, and it is as likely that he took that.'

'Then do you take one and I the other.'

'One moment, I hear the sound of hoofs!'

'Yes, yes, it is his horse!'

A great black horse, which was certainly that of General Savary, had broken out suddenly through a dense tangle of brambles in front of us. The saddle was empty.

'He has found some hiding-place here amongst the brambles,' I cried.

Gérard had already sprung from his horse, and was leading him through the bushes. I followed his example, and in a minute or two we made our way down a winding path into a deep chalk quarry.

'There is no sign of him!' cried Gérard. 'He has escaped us.'

But suddenly I had understood it all. His furious rage which the miller had described to us

was caused no doubt by his learning how he came
to be betrayed upon the night of his arrival. This
sweetheart of his had in some way discovered it,
and had let him know. His promise to deliver
himself up to-morrow was in order to give him
time to have his revenge upon my uncle. And
now with one idea in his head he had ridden to this
chalk quarry. Of course, it must be the same
chalk quarry into which the underground passage
of Grosbois opened, and no doubt during his
treasonable meetings with my uncle he had learned
the secret. Twice I hit upon the wrong spot, but at
the third trial I gained the face of the cliff, made
my way between it and the bushes, and found the
narrow opening, which was hardly visible in the
gathering darkness. During our search Savary had
overtaken us on foot, so now, leaving our horses in
the chalk-pit, my two companions followed me
through the narrow entrance tunnel, and on into the
larger and older passage beyond. We had no lights,
and it was as black as pitch within, so I stumbled
forward as best I might, feeling my way by keeping one hand upon the side wall, and tripping
occasionally over the stones which were scattered

along the path.   It had seemed no very great
distance when my uncle had led the way with the
light, but now, what with the darkness, and what
with the uncertainty and the tension of our feelings,
it appeared to be a long journey, and Savary's deep
voice at my elbow growled out questions as to how
many more miles we were to travel in this molecheap.

'Hush ! ' whispered Gérard.   'I hear someone
in front of us.'

We stood listening in breathless silence.   Then
far away through the darkness I heard the sound
of a door creaking upon its hinges.

'On, on ! ' cried Savary, eagerly.   'The rascal
is there, sure enough.   This time at least we have
got him ! '

But for my part I had my fears.   I remembered
that my uncle had opened the door which led into
the castle by some secret catch.   This sound which
we had heard seemed to show that Toussac had
also known how to open it.   But suppose that he
had closed it behind him.   I remembered its size
and the iron clampings which bound it together.
It was possible that even at the last moment we
might find ourselves face to face with an insuperable

obstacle. On and on we hurried in the dark, and then suddenly I could have raised a shout of joy, for there in the distance was a yellow glimmer of light, only visible in contrast with the black darkness which lay between. The door was open. In his mad thirst for vengeance Toussac had never given a thought to the pursuers at his heels.

And now we need no longer grope. It was a race along the passage and up the winding stair, through the second door, and into the stone-flagged corridor of the Castle of Grosbois, with the oil-lamp still burning at the end of it. A frightful cry—a long-drawn scream of terror and of pain--rang through it as we entered.

'He is killing him! He is killing him!' cried a voice, and a woman servant rushed madly out into the passage. 'Help, help; he is killing Monsieur Bernac!'

'Where is he?' shouted Savary.

'There! The library! The door with the green curtain!' Again that horrible cry rang out, dying down to a harsh croaking. It ended in a loud, sharp snick, as when one cracks one's joint, but many times louder. I knew only too well what that dreadful sound portended. We rushed together into the room, but the hardened Savary and the dare-devil hussar both recoiled in horror from the sight which met our gaze.

My uncle had been seated writing at his desk, with his back to the door, when his murderer had entered. No doubt it was at the first glance over his shoulder that he had raised the scream when he saw that terrible hairy face coming in upon him, while the second cry may have been when those great hands clutched at his head. He had never risen from his chair—perhaps he had been too paralysed by fear—and he still sat with his back to the door. But what struck the colour from our cheeks was that his head had been turned completely round, so that his horribly distorted purple face looked squarely at us from between his shoulders. Often in my dreams that thin face, with the bulging grey eyes, and the shockingly open mouth, comes to disturb me. Beside him stood Toussac, his face flushed with triumph, and his great arms folded across his chest.

'Well, my friends,' said he, 'you are too late, you see. I have paid my debts after all.'

'Surrender!' cried Savary.

'Shoot away! Shoot away!' he cried, drumming his hands upon his breast. 'You don't suppose I fear your miserable pellets, do you? Oh, you imagine you will take me alive! I'll soon knock that idea out of your heads.'

In an instant he had swung a heavy chair over his head, and was rushing furiously at us. We all fired our pistols into him together, but nothing could stop that thunderbolt of a man. With the blood spurting from his wounds, he lashed madly out with his chair, but his eyesight happily failed him, and his swashing blow came down upon the corner of the table with a crash which broke it into fragments. Then with a mad bellow of rage he sprang upon Savary, tore him down to the ground, and had his hand upon his chin before Gérard and I could seize him by the arms. We were three strong men, but he was as strong as all of us put together, for again and again he shook himself free, and again and again we got our grip upon him once more. But he was losing blood fast. Every instant his huge strength ebbed away. With a supreme effort he staggered to his feet, the three of

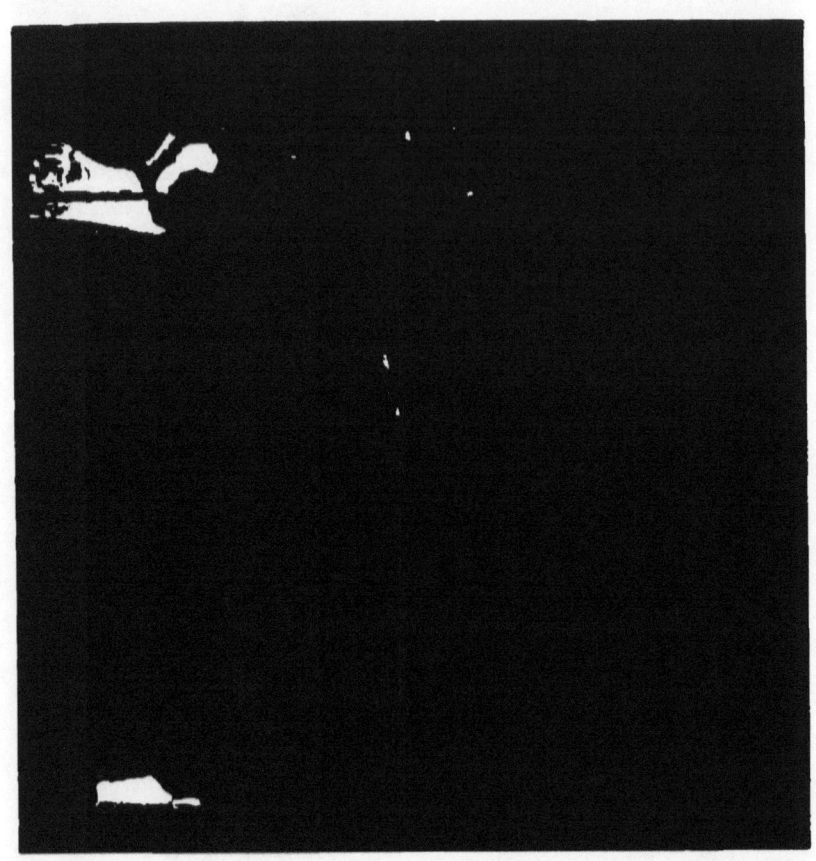

HE SWUNG A HEAVY CHAIR OVER HIS HEAD

us hanging on to him like hounds on to a bear. Then, with a shout of rage and despair which thundered through the whole castle, his knees gave way under him, and he fell in a huge inert heap upon the floor, his black beard bristling up towards the ceiling. We all stood panting round, ready to spring upon him if he should move; but it was over. He was dead.

Savary, deadly pale, was leaning with his hand to his side against the table. It was not for nothing that those mighty arms had been thrown round him.

'I feel as if I had been hugged by a bear,' said he. 'Well, there is one dangerous man the less in France, and the Emperor has lost one of his enemies. And yet he was a brave man too!'

'What a soldier he would have made!' said Gérard thoughtfully. 'What a quartermaster for the Hussars of Berchény! He must have been a very foolish person to set his will against that of the Emperor.'

I had seated myself, sick and dazed, upon the settee, for scenes of bloodshed were new to me then, and this one had been enough to shock the most hardened. Savary gave us all a little cognac from his flask, and then tearing down one of the curtains he laid it over the terrible figure of my Uncle Bernac.

'We can do nothing here,' said he. 'I must get back and report to the Emperor as soon as possible. But all these papers of Bernac's must be seized, for many of them bear upon this and other conspiracies.' As he spoke he gathered together a number of documents which were scattered about the table—among the others a letter which lay before him upon the desk, and which he had apparently just finished at the time of Toussac's irruption.

'Hullo, what's this?' said Savary, glancing over it. 'I fancy that our friend Bernac was a dangerous man also. "My dear Catulle—I beg of you to send me by the very first mail another phial of the same tasteless essence which you sent three years ago. I mean the almond decoction which leaves no traces. I have particular reasons for wanting it in the course of next week, so I implore you not to delay. You may rely upon my interest with the Emperor whenever you have occasion to demand it." '

'Addressed to a chemist in Amiens,' said Savary, turning over the letter. 'A poisoner then, on the top of his other virtues. I wonder for whom this essence of almonds which leaves no trace was intended.'

'I wonder,' said I.

After all, he was my uncle, and he was dead, so why should I say further?

CHAPTER XVII

THE END

GENERAL SAVARY rode straight to Pont de Briques to report to the Emperor, while Gérard returned with me to my lodgings to share a bottle of wine. I had expected to find my Cousin Sibylle there, but to my surprise there was no sign of her, nor had she left any word to tell us whither she had gone.

It was just after daybreak in the morning when I woke to find an equerry of the Emperor with his hand upon my shoulder.

'The Emperor desires to see you, Monsieur de Laval,' said he.

'Where?'

'At the Pont de Briques.'

I knew that promptitude was the first requisite for those who hoped to advance themselves in his service. In ten minutes I was in the saddle, and in half an hour I was at the château. I was conducted upstairs to a room in which were the Emperor and Josephine, she reclining upon a sofa in a charming dressing-gown of pink and lace, he striding about in his energetic fashion, dressed in the curious costume which he assumed before his official hours had begun—a white sleeping suit, red Turkish slippers, and a white bandanna handkerchief tied round his head, the whole giving him the appearance of a West Indian planter. From the strong smell of eau-de-Cologne I judged that he had just come from his bath. He was in the best of humours, and she, as usual, reflected him, so that they were two smiling faces which were turned upon me as I was announced. It was hard to believe that it was this man with the kindly expression and the genial eye who had come like an east wind into the reception-room the other night, and left a trail of wet cheeks and downcast faces wherever he had passed.

'You have made an excellent début as aide-de-camp,' said he; 'Savary has told me all that has occurred, and nothing could have been better arranged. I have not time to think of such things myself, but my wife will sleep more soundly now that she knows that this Toussac is out of the way.'

'Yes, yes, he was a terrible man,' cried the Empress. ' So was that Georges Cadoudal. They were both terrible men.'

'I have my star, Josephine,' said Napoleon, patting her upon the head. ' I see my own career lying before me and I know exactly what I am destined to do. Nothing can harm me until my work is accomplished. The Arabs are believers in Fate, and the Arabs are in the right.'

' Then why should you plan, Napoleon, if everything is to be decided by Fate ? '

' Because it is fated that I should plan, you little stupid. Don't you see that that is part of Fate also, that I should have a brain which is capable of planning. I am always building behind a scaffolding, and no one can see what I am building until I have finished. I never look forward for less than two years, and I have been busy all morning, Monsieur de Laval, in planning out the events which will occur in the autumn and winter of 1807. By the way, that good-looking cousin of yours appears to have managed this

affair very cleverly. She is a very fine girl to be
wasted upon such a creature as the Lucien Lesage
who has been screaming for mercy for a week past.
Do you not think that it is a great pity?'

I acknowledged that I did.

'It is always so with women—ideologists,
dreamers, carried away by whims and imaginings.
They are like the Easterns, who cannot conceive
that a man is a fine soldier unless he has a
formidable presence. I could not get the Egyptians
to believe that I was a greater general than Kléber,
because he had the body of a porter and the head
of a hair-dresser. So it is with this poor creature
Lesage, who will be made a hero by women because
he has an oval face and the eyes of a calf. Do
you imagine that if she were to see him in his
true colours it would turn her against him?'

'I am convinced of it, sire. From the little
that I have seen of my cousin I am sure that no
one could have a greater contempt for cowardice
or for meanness.'

'You speak warmly, sir. You are not by
chance just a little touched yourself by this fair
cousin of yours?'

'Sire, I have already told you——'

'Ta, ta, ta, but she is across the water, and many things have happened since then.'

Constant had entered the room.

'He has been admitted, sire.'

'Very good. We shall move into the next room. Josephine, you shall come too, for it is your business rather than mine.'

The room into which we passed was a long, narrow one. There were two windows at one side, but the curtains had been drawn almost across, so that the light was not very good. At the further door was Roustem the Mameluke, and beside him, with arms folded and his face sunk downwards in an attitude of shame and contrition, there was standing the very man of whom we had been talking. He looked up with scared eyes, and started with fear when he saw the Emperor approaching him. Napoleon stood with legs apart and his hands behind his back, and looked at him long and searchingly.

'Well, my fine fellow,' said he at last, 'you have burned your fingers, and I do not fancy that you will come near the fire again. Or do you perhaps think of continuing with politics as a profession ? '

'If your Majesty will overlook what I have done,' Lesage stammered, ' I shall faithfully promise you that I will be your most loyal servant until the day of my death.'

' Hum ! ' said the Emperor, spilling a pinch of snuff over the front of his white jacket. ' There is some sense in what you say, for no one makes so good a servant as the man who has had a thorough fright. But I am a very exacting master.'

' I do not care what you require of me. Everything will be welcome, if you will only give me your forgiveness.'

'For example,' said the Emperor. ' It is one of my whims that when a man enters my service I shall marry him to whom I like. Do you agree to that ? '

There was a struggle upon the poet's face, and he clasped and unclasped his hands.

' May I ask, sire—— ? '

' You may ask nothing.'

' But there are circumstances, sire—— '

'There, there, that is enough ! ' cried the

Emperor harshly, turning upon his heel. I do not argue, I order. There is a young lady, Mademoiselle de Bergerot, for whom I desire a husband. Will you marry her, or will you return to prison ? '

Again there was the struggle in the man's face, and he was silent, twitching and writhing in his indecision.

' It is enough ! ' cried the Emperor. ' Roustem, call the guard ! '

' No, no, sire, do not send me back to prison.'

' The guard, Roustem ! '

' I will do it, sire ! I will do it ! I will marry whomever you please ! '

' You villain ! ' cried a voice, and there was Sibylle standing in the opening of the curtains at one of the windows. Her face was pale with anger and her eyes shining with scorn ; the parting curtains framed her tall, slim figure, which leaned forwards in her fury of passion. She had forgotten the Emperor, the Empress, everything, in her revulsion of feeling against this craven whom she had loved.

' They told me what you were,' she cried. ' I would not believe them, I *could* not believe them—

for I did not know that there was upon this earth
a thing so contemptible. They said that they
would prove it, and I defied them to do so, and
now I see you as you are. Thank God that I have
found you out in time! And to think that for
your sake I have brought about the death of a man
who was worth a hundred of you! Oh, I am
rightly punished for an unwomanly act. Toussac
has had his revenge.'

'Enough!' said the Emperor sternly. 'Constant, lead Mademoiselle Bernac into the next
room. As to you, sir, I do not think that I can
condemn any lady of my Court to take such a man
as a husband. Suffice it that you have been shown
in your true colours, and that Mademoiselle Bernac
has been cured of a foolish infatuation. Roustem,
remove the prisoner!'

'There, Monsieur de Laval,' said the Emperor,
when the wretched Lesage had been conducted
from the room. 'We have not done such a bad
piece of work between the coffee and the breakfast.
It was your idea, Josephine, and I give you credit
for it. But now, de Laval, I feel that we owe
you some recompense for having set the young

aristocrats a good example, and for having had a share in this Toussac business. You have certainly acted very well.'

'I ask no recompense, sire,' said I, with an uneasy sense of what was coming.

'It is your modesty that speaks. But I have already decided upon your reward. You shall have such an allowance as will permit you to keep up a proper appearance as my aide-de-camp, and I have determined to marry you suitably to one of the ladies-in-waiting of the Empress.'

My heart turned to lead within me.

'But, sire,' I stammered, 'this is impossible.'

'Oh, you have no occasion to hesitate. The lady is of excellent family and she is not wanting in personal charm. In a word, the affair is settled, and the marriage takes place upon Thursday.'

'But it is impossible, sire,' I repeated.

'Impossible! When you have been longer in my service, sir, you will understand that that is a word which I do not tolerate. I tell you that it is settled.'

'My love is given to another, sire. It is not possible for me to change.'

'Indeed!' said the Emperor coldly. 'If you persist in such a resolution you cannot expect to retain your place in my household.'

Here was the whole structure which my ambition had planned out crumbling hopelessly about my ears. And yet what was there for me to do?

'It is the bitterest moment of my life, sire,' said I, 'and yet I must be true to the promise which I have given. If I have to be a beggar by the roadside, I shall none the less marry Eugénie de Choiseul or no one.'

The Empress had risen and had approached the window.

'Well, at least, before you make up your mind, Monsieur de Laval,' said she, 'I should certainly take a look at this lady-in-waiting of mine, whom you refuse with such indignation.'

With a quick rasping of rings she drew back the curtain of the second window. A woman was standing in the recess. She took a step forward into the room, and then—and then with a cry and a spring my arms were round her, and hers round me, and I was standing like a man in a dream, looking down into the sweet laughing eyes of my

Eugénie.   It was not until I had kissed her and
kissed her again upon her lips, her cheeks, her hair,
that I could persuade myself that she was indeed
really there.

'Let us leave them,' said the voice of the
Empress behind me. 'Come, Napoleon. It makes
me sad! It reminds me too much of the old days
in the Rue Chautereine.'

So there is an end of my little romance, for the
Emperor's plans were, as usual, carried out, and
we were married upon the Thursday, as he had
said.   That long and all-powerful arm had plucked
her out from the Kentish town, and had brought
her across the Channel, in order to make sure of
my allegiance, and to strengthen the Court by
the presence of a de Choiseul.   As to my cousin
Sibylle, it shall be written some day how she
married the gallant Lieutenant Gérard many years
afterwards, when he had become the chief of a
brigade, and one of the most noted cavalry leaders
in all the armies of France.   Some day also I may
tell how I came back into my rightful inheritance
of Grosbois, which is still darkened to me by the

thought of that terrible uncle of mine, and of what happened that night when Toussac stood at bay in the library. But enough of me and of my small fortunes. You have already heard more of them, perhaps, than you care for.

As to the Emperor, some faint shadow of whom I have tried in these pages to raise before you, you have heard from history how, despairing of gaining command of the Channel, and fearing to attempt an invasion which might be cut off from behind, he abandoned the camp of Boulogne. You have heard also how, with this very army which was meant for England, he struck down Austria and Russia in one year, and Prussia in the next. From the day that I entered his service until that on which he sailed forth over the Atlantic, never to return, I have faithfully shared his fortunes, rising with his star and sinking with it also. And yet, as I look back at my old master, I find it very difficult to say if he was a very good man or a very bad one. I only know that he was a very great one, and that the things in which he dealt were also so great that it is impossible to judge him by any ordinary standard. Let him rest silently, then, in his great red tomb at the Invalides, for the workman's work is done, and the mighty hand which moulded France and traced the lines of modern Europe has crumbled into dust. The Fates have used him, and the Fates have thrown him away, but still it lives, the memory of the little man in the grey coat, and still it moves the thoughts and actions of men. Some have written to praise and some to blame, but for my own part I have tried to do neither one nor the other, but only to tell the impression which he made upon me in those far-off days when the Army of England lay at Boulogne, and I came back once more to my Castle of Grosbois.

PRINTED BY
SPOTTISWOODE AND CO., NEW-STREET SQUARE
LONDON

www.ingramcontent.com/pod-product-compliance
Lightning Source LLC
Chambersburg PA
CBHW031341070726
47496CB00017B/1399